Mad, Rich, and Famous

Sophie Parkin's main ambition in life is to have as much fun as humanly possible. This has manifested itself in many ways throughout the years. As a rug rat it was making mud and worm pies, and as she got older she maintained her interest in cooking but added chatting and climbing trees to her array of abilities as a seasoned tomboy.

Sophie has a degree in Fine Art, otherwise known as painting, chatting, writing and partying. In between chatting, she has had two children (Paris and Carson), has had painting exhibitions, run nightclubs, written grown-up novels and for newspapers, been a kids' Agony Aunt for AOL and cooked quite a lot. She has no pets or husbands as she might be allergic to both – except for a stray cat called Cat, who loves her only for her copious gifts of milk and salmon. It is a simple one-way relationship.

This is her second teenage novel. Unlike Lily, Sophie has never passed a French exam, and has never learned to speak another language, however she does love Paris (her son and the city) and is very fond of berets and most French food that doesn't involve cow, sheep or pigs' intestines.

Mad, Rich, and Famous

the life and loves of lily

Sophie Parkin

Piccadilly Press • London

For Paris.
Richly loved, famously funny and madly handsome.

First published in Great Britain in 2006
by Piccadilly Press Ltd,
5 Castle Road, London NW1 8PR
www.piccadillypress.co.uk

A catalogue record for this book is available
from the British Library

ISBN: 1 85340 864 6 (trade paperback)
ISBN-13: 978 1 85340 864 9

1 3 5 7 9 10 8 6 4 2

Printed and bound in Great Britain by Bookmarque Ltd.
Text design by Terry Granditch, Cambridge
Cover design by Susan Hellard and Simon Davis
Set in Dante Visual and ITC Legacy

CHAPTER ONE

When Good Goes Bad

Officially Hilarious

On days when even your sister behaves like a best friend, you know everything is going to go right. It's when nobody can make a day bad, when even the milk wouldn't go off if you forgot to put it back in the fridge. Well, I was feeling just that good. *Un très bon jour* – as they might say in France.

I descended the stairs feeling downright excellent, one hand on the banister, my head held high, lipstick in place and a discreet comb of mascara across my lashes.

In my imagination I was about to receive an award – a special award, something like Ambassador of Hilarity & Kindness to the United Nations. I was floating down a marble staircase to hoards of dedicated fans, when I was rudely interrupted, typically, by Mum and Dad walking through the front door, ruining it all and shattering my dreams of world domination.

'What *do* you think you look like? Where do you think you're going? You, Miss Lily Lovitt, are not going out wearing that! Jenny, just look at your daughter. Where did she get those clothes?' said the growling, grumpy, old sweater-wearing dinosaur, otherwise known as Dad.

Then he started to really rant, full volume. 'Go back upstairs and change. No daughter of mine is going to be seen out exposing herself like that! And whilst you're about it, you can go and wipe all that muck off your face. Did you intend to make some money on the streets, or are you just trying to look like a prize —?'

'Peter!' Mum was shocked. My baby brother Bay started to cry, and even evil sister Poppy came out of her room to stare. I couldn't complain that I hadn't got an audience; it was just the wrong kind. A year ago I'd probably have burst into tears and run into my room, inconsolable, but now anything Dad says *ça glisse comme de l'eau sur les plumes d'un canard* (water off a duck's back). *Je ne m'inquiète pas!* If you know what I mean? French always sounds so much better and has the added plus of grown-ups not understanding. (If you don't know what I mean, consult the famous Lilicionary at the back of this book – all is revealed! And no, not in a picture-of-me-in-a-topless-bikini way!) I have developed a drip-dry mechanism to Dad-sarcasm.

'No, Dad. I'm going to a premiere tonight with Maya.' I have become as my dad often says, 'Tough as old boots'. I was standing my ground, hands on hips and nose to the fore, rhino-style.

'What premiere? Why don't I know anything about this?' Dad's head growls. It looks like the old croc from *Peter Pan* and just as ready to bite my head off.

And yet just before their return I'd been so happy. In fact, only minutes before, I'd written in my diary – cockahoop with joy:

Dear Diary,
Blake loves me. I know he does. He has e-mailed me lovely gorgeous kisses, eight of them (and a hug), and he said 'I was lovely'. That is all the proof I need. Oh, I can't wait to see him at half-term. He is the best boyfriend ever.
  This holiday is going to be the best of the greatest. Hope I don't get arrested for kissing his face off, it is a possibility – J'aime *Blake!*

Then Mum said patiently to Dad, 'I told you about it last night, darling.'

Darling?! What on earth was Mum calling him, Dad, 'darling' for? This was worse than I imagined. They were officially divorced . . . almost. Just because he broke up with his girlfriend, please don't say they're going to get back together now! Next thing, they'll start snogging or something equally revolting!

'What Mum means is that I am going to the premiere of the new Darrelly Brothers film with Maya and staying over at her house. Her mum and dad produced it, and they are very rich, famous and clever and they love me, Dad, just the way I am. They'd let me do and wear whatever I like. *Ils aiment moi!*'

'What are you going on about, Lily? I wish you'd stop this awful cod-French.'

I might not have understood what he was saying about French fish, but from his change of subject, I knew I had the upper hand.

'It was all arranged ages ago, wasn't it, Mum? Mum!'

Mum was wrestling Bay's wellies, to accompanying screams in C major.

'Yes, Lily. Peter, sorry, it was. Bay, hold still!'

'But yesterday didn't you say you were going to go out with Bea tonight?'

I hated it when Dad remembered my stuff. It had been awful having to tell Bea that I'd forgotten about the premiere with Maya, and listen to the disappointment in her voice, but one of the things I love about Bea is that I always know she understands me.

That's why we're best mates – I've known her and her family for ever, plus she lives round the corner so we can see each other whenever we like. Besides, we'd only planned to go to the cinema.

'I got my diaries mixed up,' I explained to him. 'I've called her and she completely understood. Everyone knows the glamour of a premiere comes before anything else.'

'"Everyone knows the glamour of a premiere comes before anything else!"' Poppy was irritatingly mimicking me.

I made a suitable face and retorted, 'Bug off back to the drains.'

She slammed her door.

'Just remind me, Jenny, why we had these animals?' said the man who tells us to call him Dad. 'Sometimes I feel like I'm Dr Doolittle in the middle of a zoo.'

It's not what Dad ever says that gets to me; it's the way he says it.

'It's worse than that.' Mum had a world weary tone and she looked exhausted. 'Peter, get a drink and sit down, or something. Can't you take up smoking again? I don't think giving up agrees with you.'

Sometimes I just love Mum; she is so officially and hilariously incorrect. It didn't even make Dad smile, though.

'Now come on, Bay, you need some food, don't you?' she said, then hollered upstairs, 'Pops, have you finished your coursework?'

There was a very girly giggle from Poppy's room.

'What's the noise coming from your room? Have you got someone in there?'

Poppy protruded her innocent face out of the room. 'No, Mum. I mean, yes, Mum; I've done my coursework already.'

She might fool Mum, but never me. Poppy was hiding another boy in her room. Mum must have misread my look for concern.

'Don't worry, Lily, darling.' She smiled. 'You look lovely. Ignore Dad. I'll take you round to Maya's in a mo.'

Car Talk

Sometimes – not often, and usually when I've given up all hope – Mum switches to an unexpected side of her character. When everything around us is mad and uncontrolled and when things threaten to explode, just sometimes she can appear completely calm and in control. It's so bizarre and far from the usual chaos that we know and love in our family home that it shocks everyone, and they just do as they're told. Mum is more unpredictable than any teenager I know, so it's not always easy to find the right time for a talk, but I knew the time

6

had come as we got into the car.

At some point when we were talking – a rare and precious thing for sisters – Poppy and I had decided that Dad spending more time at our house, and Mum and Dad being together, was nice in theory – lovely in theory, I mean, who doesn't want their mum and dad together, but this is no time to get slush-puppy soppy – it didn't work in practice. Not when it meant enduring Dad's moods at home, as well as the other less desirable qualities of Dadness. Now there was further solid proof that it was not working.

I know it seems way harsh, but somebody had to remind Mum just exactly how horrible it had been when Dad left. Mum was pregnant with Bay, and all Dad could say was that he couldn't take the pressure of another baby. Not much good exactly, saying it months *after* the baby-making event had happened. And, imagine how great it made me and Poppy feel? I suppose he went to school before they invented sex education classes, but still he should have known what made what after Poppy was born, and had it confirmed with me. Other friends of mine felt they were the reason their father left, but how could I take it personally?

Dad's departure was such a mid-life-middle-age-works-in-advertising-must-buy-a-sports-car-because-he's-going-bald thing. I remember hearing him say to

Mum in front of Poppy and me (and I promise I haven't made this up): 'Look at yourself, Jenny. How could I, or anybody, want you now that you're pregnant, fat, and have two kids? Have you looked in the mirror recently?' Poor Mum burst into tears and Dad just retorted, 'See? You're so impossibly hormonal and moody all the time. I can't deal with you. You're such a mess.' Then he stormed out the house.

So it really was our duty, Poppy's and mine, to remind Mum what he, even if he was our dad, was capable of, and what she, even if she was our mum, was capable of forgetting.

So as we sat in the car and drove over Battersea Bridge to Chelsea where Maya lived, it was time for tactics. I had to start Game Plan One: innocence.

'Mummmm?'

'Yesssssssss?' she jokingly mimicked me.

'Mummmm, welllll, you know how Dad is spending loads of time at our house?'

'Yes.'

'Do you think it's, well, healthy?'

'Lily?'

'Well, he might start to think he lives there, and then it'll be so much harder to tell him he doesn't, if you see what I mean.'

'What? Dad isn't living with us. He just likes spending

time with Poppy and Bay and, obviously, you.'

'Yes, obviously me. But, what happens when you get a new boyfriend? It was embarrassing enough with FishMan, I mean Adrien, your ex-boyfriend, still working around the corner in the café. And now with Dad around too, it'll be a nightmare.'

'What new boyfriend? Anyway, don't you want to have Dad back?'

'Well, I . . . Mum, you know how much we love you? Poppy, Bay and Me, we do really love you, and we don't want to see you go through that whole thing again. You know, when he leaves you for another secretary – you know what Dad's like. Tigers can't change their spots and neither can zebras.'

'Don't you mean stripes?'

'Whatever. Mum, Poppy and I couldn't stand it when you were miserable for so long. And who knows what long-term psychological damage it's having on Bay? Poor Bay, he's only little and sometimes he can be very sweet.'

Mum made an emergency stop just as we got to the lights. Apparently what I had said had made an impact. The silence that followed as we moved off again when the lights turned green was proof she was thinking. You can always tell when Mum is thinking because she goes all quiet; not everybody can think and talk at the same time.

I gazed out of the window as we drove through Chelsea

and past some of the most expensive houses in Britain. I love London, with all its different buildings, but most of the time I don't even stop to appreciate them. The best thing is when you look up at the tops of buildings, and that's when the unexpected things like cherubs and gargoyles or eagles and lions appear, perched, frozen in stone, just waiting to imitate life, to fly or leap. Imagine the chaos if that actually started to happen one day? All the stone and plaster statues halting the traffic, like something out of *Ghostbusters*.

Soon enough, Mum stopped the car and began to park outside Maya's.

'Lily, I have to speak to you,' she said, but she was wrestling madly with the steering wheel, and the wheel looked like it was winning. Finally the car was parked and she turned to face me and she softly held my hands in hers – which was a little weird – and said, 'It's not going to happen, darling. I mean, nothing that happened before is ever going to happen again. I promise, cross my heart. We, Dad and I, wouldn't put you, Poppy and Bay through that. It was hard on all of us, and it was our stupid fault. I'm sorry if we've been confusing you.'

'So Dad's definitely not going to move back in?'

She laughed. 'He'd better not. You know he does love you very much – that's why he can be a bit, you know, funny about your clothes. But he does love you.'

'He's got a hilarious way of showing it. He practically called me, his own daughter, a prostitute. *C'est dégueulasse!*'

'He didn't mean it. He was, well, tense, upset, stressed out. We spent all day looking for a sofa and nowhere had the right one. He's probably fine by now.'

'As long as *he*'s fine, that's the important thing. What do you think the suffragettes, and all those poor women who had to burn their bras, would think of his stropping just so he can be fine now?'

'Honestly, Lily,' said Mum, rolling her eyes. 'The two of you have got to learn to compromise. And perhaps study some history.'

Compromis, as they say in France, but not very often as, quite rightly, they are a proud race. That's just one more reason why I'm moving there as soon as I have saved enough for a one-way ticket.

'*Compromis?* When he learns the meaning of the word, then so will I, all right, Mum?'

I kissed Mum goodbye.

'OK, Lily. You are a funny sausage!' she said, shaking her head and laughing.

I hope she never calls me a funny sausage in front of Blake. It could change his whole perspective on me!

I skipped out of the car and to Maya's gate with all the lightness of a fairy. Then suddenly, thinking of Blake again, I jumped in the air and clicked my heels together

11

to celebrate. It was just like something from *Singing in the Rain*, the old Hollywood movie, but without the rain – the sky was still blue and I swear the sun came out for me at that moment.

Dad Rules

It might seem strange to other families, but life was easier without Dad. We were truly beginning to appreciate Mum's wonderfully lax and lazy ways. What does it matter if the dinner is a bit burned? At least she never grounded us, or moaned about our clothes or confiscated our MP3s. I have been keeping a recent record in my diary of Dad's Funniosities, or Fascist Rules. If you are of a delicate or nervous position look away, NOW.

1) *No eating in front of the telly. It's slobbish.*
2) *No eating along the street. It's common.*
3) *All chewing gum, banned from the house. It makes a mess.*
4) *No make-up or high heels. It's sluttish.*
5) *No eating from each other's plates. It's rude.*
6) *Bay, baby brother, must be spoiled at all times, mostly with food.*

NB: Rules 1, 2, 3 and 5 do not apply to Bay (probably 4 too).

What was Dad's problem with food? Maybe he has an eating disorder? It does make perfect sense, but can men have eating disorders? Every boy I studied at CampHappy ate like a pig, except Blake – I'm sure he ate beautifully.

I was pondering all this as I rang Maya's doorbell.

She opened the door and for a full twenty seconds we just screamed at each other with glee. Maya has this effect on me. There is something about her that wriggles into my funny bone and won't let go; it's like a comical chemical reaction – sparks fly and giggles break forth. Why is it and how is it that some people have this effect on me and others can leave me so cold and annoyed? There is such a lot of interesting stuff that scientists haven't begun to discover, and I wish they'd hurry up!

In this case, what was making us laugh was the fact that we were both wearing exactly the same TopShop dress, just in different colours. *Je ne sais pas*. We stopped screaming, and slowed into laughing.

When I caught my breath, I stuttered, 'Now, Maya, stop . . . stop it. Seriously . . . stop laughing . . . you're making me laugh too much. Look, I've got a serious question to ask you.' I took a deep breath to calm down and stop the giggles. 'Can men have eating disorders?'

At which point her dad walked past, stuffing some fat sandwich into his mouth, tapping his nine-month-pregnant stomach.

'You have to ask?' she said, and then we were helpless, crawling around on the floor, laughing.

Her father turned around and, looking at us, asked, 'Are you ready, girls, or do you need something to eat before we go?' Which just set us off again. It reminded me of the time in camp during the summer when I'd met Blake and Maya.

Blake's friend William and I couldn't stop laughing for what seemed like days. But now I couldn't think about William, because I had chosen Blake over and above him. Would I ever laugh like that with Blake? What if Blake wasn't funny? For a moment I couldn't recall if he was, and felt that I might fall off the earth if I couldn't remember. Just thinking that panicked me enough to stop laughing, pick myself up and follow Maya upstairs. He must be quite funny, I thought. I wouldn't have kissed him otherwise.

Weird Witchee Nutcase

'You look great,' said Maya, as she grabbed some nail varnish.

'So do you.'

'That's because we're wearing the same outfit!'

Almost true: except my dress was black and hers was red, our jackets were a little different, I have big curly hair and Maya has long, dark black hair, and I'm tall and she's short. Still, we could almost have been twins if it weren't for all the differences; we even had on the same red, sparkly ballet pumps on.

'I didn't know you had Dorothy shoes,' I said to her, for that was what I always called mine.

'But mine aren't. They're Toto's.'

'What are you on about?' I asked, wrinkling my nose.

'Well, you know Dorothy in *The Wizard of Oz* movie? She clicked her sparkly red shoes when she wished. Her dog was called —'

'Toto, yes. It's one of my favourite movies.'

'So, *toto*, in Spanish, means "everything". So they are my Toto wishing shoes – I can wish for everything.'

'Wow, Maya! That's great.' It might not make a lot of sense to other people, but to me it was perfect. 'Maya, have you ever suspected you might be a little head crazeee? A Wicked Witchee of the North nutcase?'

Maya looked up from painting her nails and with a completely blank face said, 'No.'

She is funny. That girl is so funny, it's not funny. She cracks me up like a broken egg.

'So? This premiere, what's it going to be like?' I asked, falling back on to her huge circular bed covered in the softest fur rug. It looked like a huge, black and white cow had been steamrollered over her bed. It wasn't a room for vegetarians.

The rest of her room is just as grand, with its flat screen TV hanging off the wall, a black leather desk with white stitching supporting the latest laptop computer and printer, matching Mickey and Minnie Mouse leather chairs – ears for back rests – and a magical white glass and mirror dressing table that shines from under the window, reflecting her collection of perfume bottles.

'What usually happens – do you think I should put on a different colour lip-gloss? – is that all the stars walk in and we get to gawp at them, and then we go and sit down, but of course they've all seen the film already so they usually wait until the lights go down and then they leave.'

'What a cheat.'

'You can't blame them really. It's probably their fifth premiere for the film that week. Lots of actors hate looking at their films, because when they do something wrong, it's ten metres high and glaringly obvious.'

'I hadn't thought of that.'

I was really impressed. Maya comes from such a glamorous and different world, sometimes I couldn't quite believe that I knew her. What amazed me was that she took it all so much for granted; the world of movie stars was normal for her. It made what Bea and I did seem so normal, and our families so boring. For me, it was almost as good as being in a movie – something I will do one day. Of course that will be after I've become a famous writer living in Paris. Maybe I could live in Hollywood and Paris? Maybe I could play the part of a writer living in Paris and film it in Hollywood . . .

'So don't bother asking them about the movie, because they probably won't remember. Mum always says actors are the most boring people ever.'

'All of them? Even the handsome ones?' I asked, amazed.

'Yup. In fact they're the worst, especially when they love looking at themselves!'

'Girls, are you ready?' Maya's mum popped her head around the corner of the door.

Maya's mum looks like a blonde movie star with all of her make-up, jewels and sink-loads of perfume. 'Hey, Lily, how are you? You look terrific! The car will be here any moment.'

'Thanks.' I smiled back at her, much to Maya's irritation.

'Mum! Would you mind knocking next time? We might have been doing something private.'

'Like what?' She sounded horrified. Like many others on this planet, she doesn't seem to understand her daughter's sense of humour.

'None of your beeswax. Now if you could please go away,' she said, dismissing her mother as if she was a servant.

'Hey, talking about going away – are you still coming to Norfolk with me? It's going to be so cool,' I said.

'I don't know. Dad said we might go away at half-term.'

'Oh, but Norfolk won't be fun without you, and you so promised. It'll be just like summer camp again, but this time we can have a riot without being dragged to the Prof's office to be told off all the time.'

'How do you know Blake's parents aren't child beaters, huh? Who's going?'

'So far it's me, you and Bea.'

A premiere was exciting, but the idea of going on another adventure with Maya to Blake's house in Norfolk was really exciting, because it would last more than one night.

'Oh, Bea.'

'Yes, Bea.'

'But she didn't go to camp.'

'But it would have been fun if she had,' I pointed out.

'But she didn't, did she?'

'*Non, mais pourquoi?*'

'I am going to ignore the fact you've forgotten English, Lily. Let's face it, if there's only Blake and you, what are Bea and I meant to do – just stand around watching you two snog? That'll be fun. Not. Why can't you go on your own?'

'I'm not going by myself! Not only would it be weird, my dad wouldn't let me and, and . . . you obviously have forgotten the meaning of FUN.'

'Lily, just because he lives in a big house doesn't mean the trip will be drop dead hilarious. Anyway big houses in the country are always freezing and haunted.'

'Don't be a *cochon*.' I was irritated by Maya, but maybe because what she was saying seemed uncomfortably close to the truth. What if it wasn't fun, but spooky and cold, and what if Blake and I couldn't think of anything to say to each other? I didn't want to think about it, and I didn't want to go without Maya and Bea, because I knew that, as long as we were all together, we could have a laugh, whatever happened.

Outside a car honked, then the doorbell rang and the bellow of Maya's dad and her mum's shrieks drenched the house.

'Maya, quick, can I borrow a lip-gloss?'

'Which one?' She opened the drawer and inside there must have been fifty varieties.

We might have been wearing the same dress, but we clearly came from different planets.

CHAPTER TWO

On The Road

Tuesday

Dear Diary,

The premiere was the most wonderful night of my life. (Yes, even more spectacular than Blake kissing me!) Walking up the red carpet, surrounded by glamorous stars and all those cameras flashing, fans screaming, women in beautiful dresses: crazeeee! Life now seems so dull. Dull, hypnotically dull! On a scale of one to ten, it reaches eleven most days. The premiere was such a fantastically exciting shade of fluorescent pink, it makes everything else look the colour of my white knickers after Mum's put them in the wash – dreary grey-pink.

Have been thinking very deeply about the speed of life.

Lily's Philosophy Of TIME

How can people even ask a question as stupid as, 'What's the time?' It's obvious there isn't one type of time; there must be at least four at any point.

1) **Stratospherically fast** *– when something really exciting is happening; when hours seem like minutes.*

2) **Fast** *– when exciting things are about to happen and your head is filled with them so you don't notice the hours. This is officially Dream Time.*

3) **Slow** *– when life is comprised just of school and revision, talking to parents and tidying up your room.*

4) **Monolithically-Ice-Age slow** *– when it's two weeks until the school holidays, and the next great event. Two weeks can often seem like a century.*

I am currently crawling through the Ice Age of time.

I am desperate, and desperately bored to tears by the bitching going on between Maya and Bea. I suspect they might not like each other – and, if this continues, wonder if I might not like them either. Whenever I say the other one's coming over and let's all do something, one of them disappears. Quels les bébés!

Then there's Mum and Dad. Mum's going mad or fou, *or* toqué, *as they say in French. Her best friend, Angela (Bea's mum) saw Dad with a 'young, mystery blonde' (oooerr!) in a restaurant. Mum is now considering dyeing her hair, losing weight and buying a whole new wardrobe. This is exciting for her, but boring for us as she tells us about it every day, and, as daylight fades, diets dissolve*

21

into chocolate face-stuffing at an Olympic standard.

Poppy is drooling over another Sammy, Tommy or Johnny – they all look the same to me – ugly buglies with greasy hair and advanced acne. Think her smell and stupidity must affect her taste and eyesight. Poor Popp. She is my sister; I don't judge her, I have to be sympathetic, but can't she do something useful, like choose some fit boys to hang about our house?

Bay is an almost three-year-old monster, with a new prodding plastic sword and matching armour, who never removes his wellies. So God help all of us.

How long can two weeks take to go by until half-term?? I need answers and I want them now! Where are you, Einstein, when I need you? How slow is the speed of light, compared to the march of desperation?

Wednesday

Bored bore boring boredom!

Wonder what Blake is thinking? Is love like being hypnotised? All I can think about is Blake. I think about him smiling, and I smile too. Last night he walked into my dreams, dressed as a postbox, and turned into a goldfish bowl, but all the fish in it had his face. What does that mean?

Could write to Blake, but must not appear too eager as e-mailed him twice today. No reply since four-thirty when all he could talk about was some old school trip.

WHAT IF HE DOESN'T LIKE ME ANY MORE?

Can't even think that, I'll be sick.

Thursday

Not writing to Blake until he e-mails me back.

HE IS AN EVIL GOAT – POSSIBLY? Possibly worse than Mr Taylor – citizenship class, who gave me a detention for punctuality – how can anyone be late for learning how to be a human being? Doesn't he understand that it is living that prepares you? OK, so spam-faced, cheese-string-haired Amanda in Year Ten might never learn.

I think Poppy has learning difficulties too. I wonder if she'll ever evolve into a human being? I know she's stolen my missing kohl eye pencil.

Sunday

Blake doesn't love me. No e-mails. So no trip. My life is over. AND school tomorrow and the detention for being 'late and cheeky'. What planet is Mr Taylor from? Being punctual is hard enough, but nice too? Can they not tell my heart is being vacuumed and grated out of my chest, when it's not melting like some overripe stinky French cheese dripping off the plate of my life. Très tragic! Why have teachers no hearts?

'Lily! Why haven't you washed up after making the cookies?'

Hark, I hear the distant wail of a mother. My mother, now screaming at me – to do what? The washing up. I ask you!

'LILY!! You heard your mother.' The gentle boom of an exploding bomb drops from Dad's lips.

Am hiding in the bath.

'Sorry, Mum, I'm in the bath.'

This is the pathetic, sad dribble of my existence.

Bea Is For Best Friend

After school on Monday, Bea waited in the library whilst I suffered my 'late and cheeky' detention. Mr Taylor wouldn't even let me do my homework. Bet he hasn't got a girlfriend. He said I had to sit and think why I was there, for a whole hour. I watched the clock and it was like having boiling oil drip on my head.

Bea and I walked to the bus stop. I was trying to discuss the best ways of committing suicide with her (we were doing *Romeo and Juliet* in English, as if my life hadn't enough tragedy), but she wouldn't agree on anything.

'I think sleeping pills, drifting off in a hot bath,' I told her.

'But what about poison? One swift glug and you're out,' she retaliated.

'Poison would be painful. You'd probably get a stomach-ache, diarrhoea and throw-up everywhere. They don't show that in the films. Not with Juliet, or Cleopatra.'

'Thank you, Lily! What if you woke up while you were drowning? Drowning is really painful – your lungs do the opposite of exploding; they implode.'

'But you wouldn't wake up because of the sleeping pills.'

'So Lily Lovitt could sleep through lungs exploding?'

'Imploding you said. Possibly, if I knew I was going to die, I'd make an effort not to wake up.'

'Why are we talking about death again? Ever since you went to that posh premiere with that stuck-up Maya, you've been depressed and depressing.'

'She's not stuck up, she's fun.'

'Well, if you like her so much, why don't you go to Norfolk with just her?'

'Because, Bea, I want *you* to come. We'll have fun. Why do you have to be jealous of her?'

'Jealous of her? That's like saying I'm jealous of a packet of marshmallows!' And she jumped in the puddle that's always by the stop, just as the bus came along.

'Ah! That's so random! For your info, Maya's not coming – she's going to Hawaii. Anyway, Norfolk's not happening. I haven't heard from Blake. He doesn't like me any more,' I said, as we got on the bus. 'Happy now?'

The conductor gave me a very odd look and replied, 'No, not really love.'

'Oh, Lily, I'm sorry.' Bea put her arm through mine sympathetically.

Unfortunately a boy from Year Seven was next to us and whispered, 'Are you two lezzers? Can I watch?'

I ignored him, but disentangled myself from Bea. 'Yes, well, you should be,' I said to her.

'How long since you've spoken?'

I wanted to say weeks – it felt that way. 'Four whole days. The last time he e-mailed me was Wednesday. That's a hundred hours, so basically a year ago.'

'Maybe he had a family crisis? His hamster or father might have been run over by the lawnmower.' We thought about this for a while.

We jumped off at our stop and began walking home.

'Things happen, Lily. Strange things happen all the time.'

I knew she was trying to comfort me but even the sky had begun to cry. Strange things did actually have a way of happening to me.

'But what would be so great to stop Blake texting or e-mailing?' I asked.

'A vampire might have invaded their home and kidnapped him to a castle in Transylvania? Or he was reliving some past life experience and he got sucked back in time, perhaps?'

I tried to imagine it.

'That would definitely stop him contacting me.'

'But maybe, Lily, you should ring. Just in case.'

'Calling's always so pushy with boys. What if I can't

think of what to say? E-mail's much easier.'

'Hhmmm. Why not e-mail him, saying that you're worried there's been an accident and that you're going to call him, because ... because it's obviously an emergency?'

'Brilliant! God, Bea what would I do without you? Will you come home and help me? We can make homemade lemonade and cookies too. Mum actually did some shopping yesterday and bought more than just Ryvita and low fat spread!'

'Sometimes mums seem to forget what their real jobs are.'

'Bea?'

'Lily.'

'Glad you're my best friend.'

'Me too.'

Sometimes Even I Can Be Wrong

I clicked on my e-mails and, much to my embarrassment, this was the first thing to appear:

Lovely Lily – Catch the 12.30 from Liverpool Street Station to Norwich Central. Change at Norwich for Hanworth.

Call me when you're on the small train and Mum and I will come and collect you.

I still can't believe you're going to be here Friday. Get here fast.

Blake XXXXX

'I think he might have recovered, "Lovely Lily",' said Bea, smirking.

'Yeah, obviously, but look how boring his last e-mail was. It hardly mentioned me; he talks more about you and he hasn't even met you!'

> Bring Bea if you want. Got to go pack now, for school manoeuvres – pretending to be soldiers, camping out and night-time orienteering, almost like camp without the fun of you, so no mobiles. Won't be able to mail for the next four days. Friday is good and I'm sure we'll get on and have a great time. I will be thinking of you, lots.
> Love Blake X

'You didn't even bother reading it all, did you?' asked Bea.

I looked at Bea's face; it was full of exasperation; it looked very similar to Mum's.

'Not exactly. I didn't want to read about boring schoolboy *manoeuvres*.'

'If you had, you'd have known he went away on a trip for four days, wouldn't you?'

'I might have.'

'Is your name Lily?'

I nodded woefully.

'And are you very S-T-U-P-I-Dduhhhh?' Bea said very slowly, as if otherwise I would not have been able to U-N-D-E-R-S-T-A-N-D!

I begged forgiveness, but she just shook her head. So I hit her with a nearby cushion. Unfortunately it was one of Mum's old ones and, after I'd biffed her a few times and she'd boffed me back with another cushion, they exploded just in time for Mum to walk in with Bay.

'Ninja!' he shrieked excitedly, running through the snow of feathers, attacking us with his plastic sword. About the only thing visible were his little red wellies as he flew through the air towards us.

Above it all was Mum's cry, 'Lily, what have you done now?'

What Class Are His Parents In?

It took Bea and me two hours to clear up every single feather. It's amazing just how many feathers they cram into two cushions, and how far each feather manages to fly when unattached to a bird.

I had told Mum about Norfolk a million times, but since all she had on her brain was exercising, dieting and getting us to clear up feathers, re-stuff cushions and sew them up, she was incapable of retaining any serious information – I was considering taking her to the garage for some major repairs: I figured her gasket had blown and the wiring definitely needed fixing.

We were just finishing feather clearing when I thought I should remind her.

'So, Mum, you know school breaks up at midday on Thursday . . .'

'Mmmm.'

'Well, me and Bea will need a lift to the train station on Friday.' There was no look of recognition in her face, so I added, 'Because we're going to Blake's, in Norfolk. You haven't forgotten, have you?'

Mum seemed suspiciously happy, once she remembered that I was going away for five days, almost the whole of half-term. A smile hovered on her lips as she said, 'Are you sure? Won't his parents mind? What do they do again? I think I should speak to them.'

'I don't know. They're just parents, Mum, you don't need to speak to them. I mean, they are really, really posh and they probably wouldn't understand you. Anyway, what would you say to them?'

'What are you saying, Lily?'

'Well, you might not understand them either. After all, during the Queen's speech on Christmas Day you always say that you can't understand what she's blathering on about, and they're practically related to her.'

'Lily, I'm speechless! I'm simply counting my blessings and am grateful that someone is willing to put up with you for five days.'

Bea and I danced about the room with Bay.

'Yippee!'

'Number, please,' Mum interrupted.

'What number? Pick a number, any number . . . Six? Ten?'

'Their phone number, Lily. *Imbécile?* Eh?'

'Mum, don't try it. You can't speak French.'

'Anyway, what are his, Blake's, parents called?'

'Their names? The Right Honourable Blake Richard Bonner. So Lord and Lady Bonner. OK?'

'Stop mucking about, Lily.' She gave me her tired and irritated look. She's been practising it so long she's very good at it now; I recognise it straight away. I could tell it was one of those conversations where I knew the whole thing was pointless because she wasn't going to believe me, whatever I said.

'Seriously, Mum, that's what they are called. Lord and Lady Bonner. I told you they were posh! They live on an estate called Blakensold and, no, it's not a council estate! *Ils sont très magnifiques!* Apparently.'

And then she did believe me. I could tell by the way her mouth dropped open, like a big bin, but all she could say was, 'Oh!'

And They Call Us Teenagers

Mum picked up the phone to Bea's mum and had an intense squealing conversation as she summoned her over so they could make the phone call together. And they call us teenagers!

Bea and I didn't know whether to die of embarrassment at them being so childish, or laugh at them being so ridiculous. It took her hours to dial and when she did I wished she hadn't. Bea and I looked at each other in torturous disbelief. I hated hearing Mum put on her fake posh accent and then go all giggly before passing the phone to Angela. I could tell she was talking to a man, you always can with Mum: her voice goes abnormally squeaky and weird, even if it's just the postman.

Afterwards, Mum and Angela sat in the kitchen drinking a box of wine and laughing in a dirty way together, whilst we were starving for dinner. In the end we couldn't wait any longer and made our own. We even made some pasta for Bay.

'I see why you like Blake. His father's got a very sexy voice,' Mum said, then laughed like an unblocking drain.

'*Maman, tu es répugnante.*'

'It's true, I heard it. It was all deep and gravelly.' Angela giggled and Mum grunted, like a pig, full of laughter and choking in her wine.

Bea and I looked at each other and went into the living room for some peace and quiet, to eat and plan. That lasted for about five minutes before the inevitable shout of, 'Where's Poppy?' swiftly followed by, 'Lily, doll, if you're going away, how about giving Bay a bath and a bedtime story? I'll give you spending money for Norfolk.'

I'm so easily bribed where money is concerned. I only hope Mum remembers in the morning.

Tuesday

Dear Diary,

Only two more days to go, before I have to pack.

Life is soooo exciting. Three texts and an e-mail from Blake, all calling me Lovely Lily (and sometimes just LL for short – clever and funny). Soon I will be melted marshmallows in his arms, all toasty sweet, gooeylicious and warm. Fried through with all the happiness that Cassandra felt in I Capture the Castle (fav number one book), when Simon, with all his 'fine lines', first kissed her. Luckily Blake isn't going out with Poppy, like Simon was with Cassandra's sister, Rose. Now that would be complicated. I wonder if kissing Blake now will be as nice as the first time. Help! What if I've gone off him? What then? I don't think I can remember exactly what he looks like. What if I don't recognise him at the station and we get stranded in Norfolk? I'm mad. No, I'm sure it will all be fine.

Pack Up Your Troubles

Thursday after school, Bea and I ran home from the bus stop in a fit of feverish excitement.

'To pack properly, really, I need to move the whole of my bedroom into yours,' I decided. 'Or, yours into mine?'

'How about we take the phones into our bedrooms

and talk whilst we pack, then at least we'll know exactly what we've got to take between us.'

'Brilliant, Bea, but meanwhile there are important questions to be answered. Ugly or practical? I mean wellies: yes or no?'

'Traditionally, yes, for the countryside. But it hasn't rained for months.'

'It rained when we were coming home from school the other day.'

'For five minutes. Anyway I checked the weather conditions in Norfolk on the Internet. Dry.'

'So, no. Raincoat? Swimsuit? Goggles and flippers? How many pairs of shoes and evening dresses? What if there's a grand ball or a beach party?'

'Text Blake and ask him if you should bring: 1) swimsuit; 2) ball gown; 3) jumper – it sometimes gets very cold in the country at night, which is just one reason why civilised people live in cities.'

And so we went off and packed. One hour and seven minutes later I got a return text from Blake.

1) No – bikini. 2) No – mini-skirt. 3) Yes – 3.

How could I have doubted that Blake was funny? Of course he is. Unless he was being serious. Three jumpers? It must be like the Arctic; Bea was right.

'Do you think a hoodie counts as a jumper? What about cardigans?' I asked Mum over dinner, who shook her head in despair and then gave me a special Mum look. She obviously didn't know the answers either. Wondered if I should Google it.

Strange Girls On A Train

'Can you believe it? We're on the train!'

'Finally!'

For a while, Bea and I just sat across from each other, smiling, our heads leaning against the window. I was enjoying the feeling of leaving everything behind – London, parents, school and the boredom of our daily lives. But what was most lovely was leaving the screaming chaos of Mum, Dad and Bay, though strictly speaking Bay wasn't part of the argument. Bay just added to the noise level once it began.

'I thought they'd never stop arguing. Sorry about my parents,' I said.

'Just wish my mum hadn't got drunk and told yours about the mystery blonde last week.'

'Do you think it really could have been what Dad said – a blond boy from the office who works for him?'

'My mum's eyesight *is* quite bad, and worse when she drinks, but we don't know whether she had been drinking when she saw them. She once spoke to a lamp-post for five minutes before realising it wasn't Uncle

Matt, so it might have been a boy. Mind you, Uncle Matt does look like a lamp-post.'

'I can't quite believe that my dad would make up such a crappy lie; like anyone would believe that.'

'I hope they didn't get arrested.'

'Who? My dad and the boy?'

'No, your parents, just now.'

'Serves them right if they did. Honestly how old are they? Fighting in the middle of the station platform in broad daylight.'

'I thought the police were going to stop us catching the train. Bay's sword didn't help much.'

'Bay's sword never does, and Mum shouldn't have grabbed it and tried to cut off Dad's head.' The whole scene was too depressing to dwell on. I was happy to be travelling quickly away. 'Look, Bea! I've spotted the first cow – we're in the country!' I said, diverting my thoughts and, I hoped, Bea's.

'It doesn't count. It's not a real cow – it's a picture of one on the side of a van. We're still in the suburbs. You are officially disqualified, and as I am the only other player, I am the winner. Hurrah!'

'Boo hiss. I'm going to have some chewing gum and read my book for a bit. Do you really think Blake will like this outfit? Or do you think I should change?'

I was wearing my new black drainpipe jeans which,

though a little hot since the weather was pretending to be summer, went so well with my pale lemon T-shirt and matching ballet shoes that it would have been rude not to wear them.

'I refuse to discuss your outfit again, Lily. Four times is enough. You're not still reading that boring *I Caught a Cottage*, are you?'

'If you mean, my little illiterate friend, *I Capture the Castle*, yes, and it's my third time. Have you got the *Quite Starving Caterpillar* book, so you can look at the pictures of what he eats?'

'Ha ha. Actually I've really got into Agatha Christie's *Poirot*.'

'Crikey, does she know? Just your type: fat, old, Belgian and with a moustache.'

'At least it's a proper adult book.'

'*Imbécile!*' I said.

'You're just saying that cos your mum did the other night. You're unnaturally obsessed with the French.'

I couldn't say anything. Damn that girl, she was right again. I didn't know what it meant, but it wasn't worth arguing about at the beginning of our holiday. I gave her one of my special looks of blatant disapproval; what else could I do?

We sat and read in silence. I was only a little annoyed at Bea's jibe. She could be very competitive in a petty way sometimes, but mostly Bea was Bea and I loved being with her. She is a good friend, my best friend, even if she could annoyingly read my mind. She kicked me on the sole of my foot and looked at me suspiciously.

'Oi, you. I know what you're thinking. Get over it.'

I had to laugh, because I knew what she was thinking too. With Maya I was constantly surprised; with Bea, I just knew.

Life would be dull without Bea, even if she did make annoying comments. *C'est la vie,* eh? And there is nothing anyone can say, not Bea, not Maya, no one, that alters the fact that French is the most beautiful language ever invented and the French are the most civilised of humans. Anyone who could invent a *pain au chocolat* and insist children eat it for breakfast gets my allegiance.

Almost There

There is nothing that looks like real, proper countryside in London, and sometimes even when you're in the country, it doesn't really feel real. It takes staring out of a train window to see all the sweeps and folds of hills swallowing you in and forests eating your tracks; the white and grey clouds fluffed up against the big blue sky; the sun glinting on water, birds flying over and out of the hedgerows, wide-winged geese dive-bombing lakes, and all the sheep tied to the grass by their mouths, scattered in the green fields, like daisies on a garden lawn. Then the only modern things are great big black pylons to remind you that a dinosaur isn't about to step through the marshes to claw you up.

'That's your phone, isn't it?' Bea said, interrupting my thoughts. I ransacked my pockets to stop an embarrassing tune; Poppy had been interfering again. Ah, that Poppy. What would I be without her? Rich? Famous? Sane?

'Hey, Maya. How are you, old thing? Oh I'm good. Yeah, on the train. Yes, it's great. I know. Well, next time, eh? Did your parents get the thank you card I sent? Good. Oh yes! Stop the beef! As if. No way. Just for you, baby. Big love. Oh I will, don't you worry.' And I laughed and laughed, shutting my phone.

Bea was pretending not to listen, but I can tell when her ears are wigging – they twitch.

'Was that Maya?' she said.

'Yes, she's sorry she's not coming with us.'

'Really. What's she doing instead, jetting off to the moon?'

'No, I told you – Hawaii.'

'*Aloha*!' She raised her eyebrows and wiggled her hands and head in a fake hula dance.

'I know,' I said, joining in. Maya lived the expensive version of our life, but it didn't mean she had more fun.

'Hey, Bea, do you want a sandwich?' I asked and

offered her one her mum had made for her.

She smiled. 'Are you sure you don't mind? It's dreadfully kind of you.'

'Not at all. What's yours is mine.'

'And what's mine is yours, obviously?'

'Exactly. I can see we're going to get along famously. I hope Blake's got a friend,' I said, because I wanted Bea to know that I was thinking of her more than Maya, or even Blake.

'I hope so too. It would be sad if you were going out with a Billy No Mates.'

'I didn't mean that. I meant for you. Bea, we're going to have a great time.' I was trying to be jolly, and I was succeeding. 'I can feel it in my waters.'

'Yuck! Go to the loo, the conductor's coming.'

'Ha ha yady-yady,' we said in unison.

CHAPTER 3

Meet The Parents

Who? What? Argh!

'Lily, is that him?'

'Of course it's him – hide!'

'Why?'

'He might see us!'

'And?'

I had to share my fear; I couldn't contain it any longer.

'Bea, help me! Blake . . . he doesn't look the same. Oh no, I think I've got the wrong boy.'

I realised the awful truth as the sun was setting prettily over the toy-town-style station. We were pulling into Hanworth.

'Lily!' Blake shouted out as he ran towards me. 'Let me get that for you.' He grinned wildly and pulled at my bag as I got off the train.

I could hardly look at him. Reality can be shocking when you've been dreaming wide awake for so long. There was nothing about him that reminded me of him. I must have given him a total make-over in my head during the past couple of months.

'You must be Bea. Can I get your case for you?'

'Hi, Blake. Thanks, sorry it's a bit heavy.'

'So, Lily? You're here. You look fantastic.' He was staring at me. 'Bea, doesn't she look great?'

'Oh, Lily always looks good,' she replied. I could feel them both staring at me, as I examined the ground.

I couldn't bear it. I knew I had to look at him and speak to him.

'Blake, eh!' I said.

'How are you?' he asked expectantly.

What could I say? The awful thing was I could see his face was all lit up, excited, his vivid hazel eyes sparkling. Everything had changed, and all I could say was, 'Good. Yes, excellent.'

Then I couldn't avoid it a minute longer. 'So, Blake, when did you get your hair cut?' I asked, when what I really meant was, 'Why, oh why, did you let someone savage your head?'

'I know it's awful, isn't it? Sorry. They did it for army training. Hopefully it won't take too long to grow back. I hate it. Look, Lily, I quite understand if you want to go back to London; I'll just take you and your case to the other platform. I'm sure a train will come along in the next day or two.'

I could tell he was joking, but I was seriously considering it. How was I going to spend the next hour with someone who didn't look like Blake, let alone days? The whole of his face looked different. It was all so wrong. I didn't feel I was talking to the same person – he looked like a skinhead. Where had all his lovely, long curls gone to? He could have at least cut one off and sent it to me in a locket to wear around my neck, like in Victorian times.

'Don't be silly,' I said, unable to take my eyes off his scalp.

'It's not that bad,' said the nice Bea. 'It suits you. Besides, it's only hair.'

I could've kicked myself for having droned on and on about him for so long to Bea. I wondered if she was secretly laughing until I felt her glare at me to pull myself together. But what was I to do? I couldn't help the way I felt, could I?

As Blake motioned us along the platform and down to the car park, thoughts of escape invaded reality – being airlifted out by a handy helicopter, or a passing sports car zipping me and Bea away. I would even have considered hopping on a donkey if there'd been one in a nearby field, until he said, 'Mum, this is Lily and Bea. Lily and Bea, this is Mum.'

And there was Lady Bonner, looking like she'd just married Prince Charles, covered in pale green tweed with an excited black Labrador jumping at her heels. Her hat looked like a pheasant had just landed on her head – no wonder the dog was jumping up. I suddenly didn't know what I was supposed to do – curtsey? Or was that just the Queen? Why didn't they ever teach you anything useful at school?

'Hello, Lady Bonner, very nice to meet you.'

'Call me Cassie, it's easier. Well, great to have you both on board and any friend of Blake's is obviously another member of the family to me. Let's get into the car.'

She opened up the doors of a huge, black four-wheel-drive Land Rover parked close by. It was the kind of car Bea personally blames for global warming and I object to for taking up so much space on the roads in London when I'm on my bike. I felt treacherous climbing into it, but it *was* lovely inside with all its soft black leather. Bea and I sat in the back. Blake was climbing into the front when his mum asked, 'But where's Poppy?'

'At home,' I replied. Surely they hadn't expected my sister? I'd only told Blake nasty things about her.

'What?' asked Lady Bonner.

'Poppy. My sister?'

'No, the dog.'

'Sometimes she behaves like a dog,' I admitted, 'but . . . Oh.'

And we all laughed, which helped to stop me thinking about being sick from the now overwhelming smell of leather. Poppy, the dog, was found and put in the boot and then off we drove. I think Blake's mum could tell we were a bit nervous, so she chatted and asked us questions about London and our school. She laughed a lot at odd little jokes she made, so it was a bit like being with my mum. I wonder if it's an age thing? I hope I don't start getting odd when I get old. I looked at Blake and tried to imagine fancying him, but I couldn't even think how I could have snogged him before.

They Call It Home?

It was about fifteen minutes before we headed off the main road and drove down a smaller, rough lane then under a great brick arch and past a gatehouse, the car rumbling over the deer grate and into a huge park.

The light was quietly seeping away, but as we drove past you could still see a herd of deer grazing, their antlers engraving the sky, and a lake surrounded by ducks, with swans gliding regally on it and sheep grazing everywhere that wasn't occupied by anything else. Do the sheep really believe they've inherited the earth? In the middle of all this countryside sat a huge, sandy-bricked museum, crowning the land. It was like something from a biscuit-tin painting.

'I've got a jigsaw puzzle that looks just like that museum,' I said.

'So have we.' Lady Bonner laughed for no apparent reason. 'Jolly hard, isn't it? And I see it every day!'

What was she talking about? Does she do jigsaws every day?

'Is your house far?' asked Bea politely.

I could tell she was obviously dying to go for a pee by the way she kept crossing her legs. She refused to go on the train – Bea's funny about lots of things like that.

'Almost home,' Lady B said, swerving around the side of the museum before braking dramatically and parking around the back of it. 'Well, here we are.'

Then it dawned on Bea and me, as we walked through the back door and stared up into the massive hallway. What we thought was a museum was in fact their idea of a home. How can I describe it? It simply looked like the poshest, biggest house I'd ever seen, let alone been inside. It obviously *was* the building on my jigsaw puzzle!

In the hall there were huge paintings encased in ornate gold frames of some of the ugliest people in fancy dress I'd ever seen, a *magnifique* staircase (with far better

46

banisters than CampHappy for sliding down), a vase of flowers that was so gargantuan it wouldn't have fitted into our kitchen at home, let alone the table on which it was standing, which was the size of our entire back garden.

'Do you girls want to go up to your room while I see how the dinner is? Dinner's at seven-thirty in the dining room. Be a good boy, Blake, and show them to rooms Blue and Green. You don't mind being in separate rooms, do you? It's just we don't have any twin beds apart from in Blake's room.' And she laughed again. *Très bizarre!*

'Come on, I'll show you around,' said Blake, smiling as if everything was normal. Bea and I looked at each other.

Rooms With Ghosts

When I opened the door to my room, I saw immediately why two beds would have been an impossibility in there: the four-poster bed could have fitted half my class in it; the bed was bigger than my bedroom.

I didn't want the Green Room because of the weird sickly portrait on the wall. I didn't care who it was by, I was not sleeping with that in the same room as me. It was way too spooky. Unfortunately Bea felt exactly the same.

'A compromise is going to have to be reached.' Blake was being most diplomatic.

'Yes,' we said simultaneously, 'and she is going to have to make it.'

We both laughed.

'Just dump your stuff. You can sort it out later. Come up to the nursery,' Blake said casually.

'Why?'

'Cos that's my den.'

I knew there was something odd about him and his haircut, but this proved it. 'You sleep in a baby nursery?'

'I'd forgotten how, well, how basic you are, Lily. No, it's just called that, silly.'

Silly?! How dare he sound like my dad, I thought.

'It's where generations of my ancestors have grown up,' he explained, leading the way.

'But they're not there now, right?' I asked.

'Duh! Ancestors aren't still going to be around,' said Bea. Whose side was she on?

'Of course they're not, they're all dead,' said Blake, confused.

'*Exactement.* My point precisely. Ghosts!' Because it may well be all very nice to go to grand old posh houses, but nobody mentions if ghosts are resident.

'Bea, you seem sensible.'

Blake was obviously guessing. 'Looks can be very deceptive,' I said. I thought it was worth mentioning.

'Oi, you!' said Bea.

'Are you afraid of ghosts, Bea?' asked Blake, putting on a deadly serious voice.

'Not so that it gets in the way of daily life, like being afraid of spiders or heights. It doesn't stop me going to school in the mornings either, unfortunately.'

'But you believe in them.'

'Of course she believes in them, Blake,' I interrupted. 'Who wouldn't, when they so clearly exist. You can practically see them leaping out of the walls here. Look, there goes another one.' I pointed into the air, my arm swooping like an owl over Blake's head as we all walked down a very long corridor.

'Er, Lily, lovely or not, please don't disturb the normal people in the house,' Blake said, grabbing my arm and frogmarching me up an awful lot of stairs.

One Nursery, No Babies

At the top, Blake opened the door to a separate landing with three rooms. One of them was enormous, quite the most *formidable* of modern rooms. Huge floor-to-ceiling French windows going on to a roof terrace with palm trees and bamboo furniture. His room was crammed full with a widescreen TV, a drum kit, an electric guitar, a computer on a desk, turntables, CD and DVD players; *bonté divine*! He even had a mini fridge next to his sofa. It was almost a flat – he also had a bathroom and a walk-in wardrobe. All that was missing was a kitchen.

'This is amazing,' I breathed.

'It's the coolest room I've ever been in,' agreed Bea.

'And I haven't even shown you the lighting effects, baby. You want me to dim the lights? Come here, Lily,' he said spookily. I had the distinct feeling he was laughing at me; he was certainly raising his eyebrows in a curious way.

Bea coughed loudly, and if she hadn't, I would have.

Blake's expressions could be very odd sometimes. I just had to keep reminding myself of how lovely some of his e-mails were. He put on MTV and we all watched for a bit, and shared a ginger beer.

A little while later, he turned it off and said, 'Downstairs you two. Time to get ready for dinner.'

'You are joking, aren't you?' I demanded.

'No.'

'I didn't bring any long dresses,' said Bea, nudging me.

'Don't worry, you can wear the really short ones.' Blake laughed hysterically. 'No, but seriously: no jeans at dinner, because we're eating in main hall. It's just one of my parents' weird rules. Can you find your room? I'll meet you in the downstairs hall when the gong goes.'

Do You Fancy Him?

'Blimey,' Bea said, once we were headed in what we hoped was the direction of our rooms.

'*Sacré coeur!*' I agreed. 'I'm sorry, Bea, forgive me. I've made you come to some odd boy's house in the middle of nowhere, he's not even good-looking and he wants us to dress for dinner! What was I thinking about?'

'You can't go off him, Lily.'

'Can't I? He looked so good with curly hair.'

'No. Not just because of a haircut,' said Bea sternly, as we walked back to the Blue Room.

'Oh.' I knew she was right. Again.

'So this is another one of your fine messes you've got us into, huh?' she said, putting on a funny Laurel and Hardy voice and making me laugh. 'And I don't even know where your room is.'

'We could both share the Blue Room,' I suggested, opening the door.

'Just in case things go bump in the night?' asked Bea.

'Yes, I'm not sleeping by myself. There's probably spirits, as well as ghosts, plus a few poltergeists too. Go away, we're here tonight,' I said, clearing the room with a shout.

'Lunatic!' Bea mocked me.

We emptied our bags on to the bed to find something to wear, and as I went through mine Bea tried the doors in the room. One was scarily locked and another led into a colossal wardrobe, so big you could have walked inside it and found Narnia at the other end, but the last was best.

'Come and look at this,' she said.

The bathroom was huge, with two great big Victorian baths facing each other, and an amazing wooden throne as a loo. It was the sort of bathroom you wouldn't mind living in.

'I think I'm going to wear my blue polka dot dress to go with the room. It's the smartest thing I've got with me,' I said.

'But what are we going to wear on the other nights? Why didn't he tell us we were going to have to dress up every night? That was really mean of him, Lily.'

'Totally. He probably takes it all for granted. Bea, what do you honestly think of Blake?'

I had been worried at the thought of having to deal with Bea and Blake not liking each other, but now how *I* felt was difficult enough.

'I think he's probably a bit nervous, but he's OK.'

'OK! Nothing else?'

'All right then, he's quite fit.'

'You don't fancy him, do you?' I felt paranoia creeping over me like some fast-growing ivy. What was worse? Them hating each other, or liking one another rather too much? I knew the answer before the question had formed in my brain, and it meant I must have still liked Blake. After all, Bea might just have been Bea to me, but to the rest of the world she was very pretty with the most amazing figure, as well as smart and funny. I could feel like such a klutz next to her if a boy was around. Too clumsy, too loud, always too silly Lily. And hadn't Blake said that?

'I've said the wrong thing, haven't I?' asked Bea quietly.

'Well . . .'

'I can't win with you, Lily. You want me to fancy him, so that you feel that you've made the right choice, but you don't want me to fancy him, in case I steal him.'

'As if you would? But you wouldn't, right?'

'Minutes ago you didn't even like him.'

'But that was minutes ago. Things change – you always say that.'

Bea looked at me as if I was the most impossible person in the world, and then laughed.

'Honestly, Lily! Of course I'll steal him, unless you let me borrow your red espadrilles – they'll go perfectly with my red and white stripy shirt. Do you think jean skirts count as jeans?'

'No, that's a skirt, though not much of one. Actually, it could probably pass as a large belt. Maybe it's a skelt.'

'Ha blimmin' ha! *Très amusant*, as you'd say.'

Just as we'd finished getting dressed and were still trying to find our earrings, the gong went.

'Modom, dinner is served,' I said in my poshest tone.

'Help! Where's my hairbrush! Was that your text alert beeping or mine?' Bea asked.

'I'll look later,' I said, glancing down at Maya's name lit up on my phone; I wasn't going to mention it now and spoil the mood.

Lord Toad Of Toad Hall

We struggled out of our stately room, left in a right state – probably more bedraggled than it had ever known.

Blake's eyebrows went up as we came down the stairs, transformed. 'You look very nice, very nice indeed!' he said, staring at Bea's long brown legs, his eyes going up and down them like a damn elevator. I hadn't planned for this happening at all, not one bit.

'Thank you,' she simpered. I stared daggers at the two of them. I should have known it. She owns the shortest skirt in the Northern hemisphere. What was she trying to do? And why was he so easily distracted?

'This way, ladies,' he said pretentiously, and led us through into a terribly grand old living room. There was gold and mirrors splashed everywhere, and not a comfortable sofa in sight. Mum wouldn't have liked that. At the fireplace stood Lady B and a man I assumed was Lord B. Both were wearing jeans. Blake sniggered because, on closer examination, so was Blake.

'Hello, girls. Darling, this is Bea and Lily. Don't you both look nice. It's not a formal dinner, you know. We haven't got other guests until tomorrow and then you can all eat in the kitchen, if you want.'

'Oh, it's nothing, we always dress for dinner at home,' I replied, whilst doing my Wonder Woman stare of destruction at Blake. Technically this was not a lie; Mum always insists that we wear clothes, so we're not naked when we're eating.

'Sorry, I didn't quite get your names,' Lord B said to us. 'You may call me Dick, or Toad, like beep beep, Toad from *The Wind in the Willows*. I like to collect cars too, poop poop. I'm Blake's father.' He was shaking a clearly petrified Bea's hand and staring at her, the way a snake stares at a mouse before dinner, then he turned and grabbed me. 'So, young lady, do you like the river bank, or are you one of the Wild Wooders, hmm?' he asked, and his eyes went all wide and googly at me. He had a huge moustache that turned up at the ends when he grinned, and orange sideburns, and hair that looked like it wanted to escape his head. I wished he wouldn't grin so; it was scary.

'Oh, you mustn't mind Dick,' said Lady B, laughing. 'Would you care for a little sherry or a shandy like Blake?'

'You don't have to be mad to live in Blakensold, but it certainly helps, eh, Pa?' quipped Blake.

'Quite so, my lad, quite so,' Lord B barked, slamming a hit on Blake's back that I would have been glad to personally deliver.

Then a man, introduced as Graham, the housekeeper, came in and said that dinner was ready, so we filed down the hall and into the dining room.

Bea grabbed my finger and squeezed it very hard. I tried to give her a convincing smile, but fear might just have got the better of me.

What had I got us into? Some bonkers spooky house of toads? How would we ever escape? And where was the odd passing helicopter when you needed it? If we ever got out of this alive I decided I would never leave home again.

'Mum, if you're telepathically listening – I do love you, Mum, I do,' I thought as hard as my mind could.

CHAPTER FOUR
All In A Day's Madness

Knock Knock?

Blakensold, Norfolk
Dear Diary,
Pour l'amour de Dieu! *This is one of those moments when only French will do. Or do I mean,* Mon Dieu! *Anyway, it's something to do with God. I have had to spend most of the night praying. Who else can you pray to when you don't feel it's Casper the Friendly Ghost who intends to pay you a visit?*

I am writing this in order not to fall asleep and be tormented by the living dead, you can never be too sure who's out there after all that I've seen in movies.

GO AWAY I DON'T BELIEVE IN YOU!

I have to keep positive. Bea has fallen asleep. How can anyone sleep at a time like this? DEAR GOD, PLEASE PROTECT AND SAVE US.

I'm sure I can cope with this; I am quite courageous. At dinner I spoke TWICE to Lord B – a man so mad that it's a good thing he locks himself away here. You wouldn't want him running around Battersea without a lead; he'd end up in Battersea Dogs Home, howling with the rest of them. Now I know why it's called barking mad, though perhaps he's more croaking mad – he thinks he's Toad of Toad Hall. I even heard him answer the phone saying, 'Hello, Toad of Toad Hall.' Is that normal? Lady B is v. nice in a v. posh way. You couldn't expect her to understand the real world, but if you gave her a problem, you know she'd try to understand, like the Queen. Lord B just wouldn't know where to start. As for Blake . . .

Oh Blake, Blake Blake Blake. I like writing his name, it makes him a bit more real. I'm not sure who he is at the moment. I mean, of course I know, but apart from him saying 'Lovely Lily', tricking us at dinner and thinking I'm unhinged (don't think he's in any position to decide after meeting his dad), I'm not sure. Is madness hereditary? Or like a cold? Could I catch it?

Now I realise my dad is not at all mad: he's just boring. Quite a relief, yet a little disappointing too.

Is Blake interesting?

Blake Blake Blake, where was I? Yes, he kept looking at Bea's legs. V. bad. Très mal. Mal extraordinaire! *Whether I like him or not, it's v. rude!*

Bea, who's sleeping in this bed and who I'm protecting by staying awake and keeping the ghouls away. And she's snoring, oblivious; typical. Tout banal.

I have not had one second alone with Blake, not a chance of a bisou, bécot *let alone a* patin! *I know I didn't like the look of him (his hair* est très savage*), but not being sure he loves me makes me furious. Maybe he loves Bea and her legs more; she has got a lot of leg – not like a spider, just compared to my trotters, I mean.*

A tree keeps knocking on the window, making a scratching sound like, like a witch's claw! Well I am defo NOT one of those idiot girls in horror films who goes to investigate. NO way! I'm not stupid. I'm hiding under the covers and playing dead until the nasties disappear.

Have tried to wake Bea, but she's still snoring. There's creaking in the corridor, I can hear a voice calling my name, oh my God. That's it . . .

Rise And Shine

'Lily, wake up! It's ten o'clock. You've been asleep for hours and I'm starving. I've even had to eat your emergency KitKat, and you know how I hate them.'

I groaned and sat up in bed, but still couldn't see her.

'That's funny,' said Bea, giggling. 'You must have fallen asleep on top of your book – half of it's printed on your face.'

There's nothing like some humiliating laughter to get you out of bed faster than a racoon with its tail alight.

I ran into the bathroom and scrubbed my face clean, but there was nothing I could do about the weird crease over my eye where the book's spine had imprinted on my skin. I made a mental note to keep my face permanently in profile for the whole day. If only I had Bay's pirate's patch. Damn! The one time that brother comes in handy, he's a hundred miles away. I could only think that, terrified from all the weirdness of the ghostly noises, I had fallen asleep through pure fear, maybe fainted even, with my diary over my eyes to shield me from the horror. I felt lucky I woke up alive.

Now the sun was shining beautifully in one of those days you dream about after the darkness of a long night. Even though it's October, it must be an Indian summer. The sky was washed a deep forever blue, the tiniest of feather-traced white clouds wafted too lazily to form into anything more threatening than lace. Outside in the deer park, the lake sparkled like a giant crystal behind the trees, the grass was greener than any grass in the history of all grass and all things green; the sheep even looked like they'd been in the washing machine.

'Bea, how come you're not even dressed?' I was tearing around the room, pulling clothes out of the drawer, dressing faster than a rabbit before a greyhound.

'And good morning to you too, Lily. I was actually doing some yoga to keep my stomach pangs from exploding, waiting for Your Majesty to wake up.'

'I was wondering what you were doing standing on your head, other than trying to find a new way to think. You shouldn't have left me awake last night.'

'Ha ha, so who forced the sleeping pills down your neck, the Boogieman?'

'What? It was you who had the sleeping pills. I couldn't sleep at all last night. I stayed up to keep guard and I was writing my diary, trying to keep my mind off all the creatures haunting us, but then I heard a witch scratching at the window asking to be let in and my name being called. You know, Bea, I must have fainted from fright.'

'Or maybe you were dreaming it all?'

'No. I'm telling you this might be the most haunted house in England.'

And just then, as if to prove my point, there was a knock at the door, not once, but twice. I stood still, staring petrified at Bea, who was still balancing on her head.

'Ghosts don't happen during the day, do they?' I whispered. Bea righted herself and we both crept behind the door.

It knocked again, and then a voice boomed, 'Lily?'

We shrieked and clung to each other, then the voice became louder and more insistent than before. 'Lily! You must be awake. Lily, if you don't get up, there'll be no breakfast left.'

It was clearly Blake. We groaned in relief. I let him in because I was dressed, but Bea scuttled into the bathroom like a cockroach glimpsing light.

'You could have said it was you. We thought it was another ghost.' Then I shouted to Bea. 'Hey, Bea, I'll meet you downstairs in the dining room. I'll grab you some breakfast, OK?' My pure greediness was overwhelming everything else. I was not missing breakfast, not for anyone. It is, after all, the most important meal of the day.

'What are you talking about? What other ghosts?' Blake looked perplexed.

Pretending he didn't know indeed!

'Can't you wait for me?' asked a mournful Bea, through the bathroom door, clearly suddenly believing in the unbelievable.

'It's only downstairs.'

'OK, fine. Go. Leave me to be attacked by ghouls.'

'But you said they don't exist.'

'They don't! Bug off!'

Breakfast Is Served

I hoped Bea wouldn't go into one of her famous 'I'm sulking' drama moods. I love Bea, but she can make a drama out of a biscuit. She narrows her eyes, flounces her hair and off she goes. Fine when it's at a teacher like Mr Taylor, but terrible when it's at me.

As Blake and I were walking downstairs I noticed something: Blake was looking rather gorgeous. His hair must have grown in the night. How had he done it? He'd got a green T-shirt on, which made him look quite fit, with jeans, and maybe I was even getting used to his hair. I needed to think about this.

I was just busy looking at him and thinking this as we walked down the corridor, when he suddenly pulled me behind a long curtain. I fell backwards into it, part shrieking, part laughing as he kissed me.

'Got you at last, Lily. I've been waiting months for this – thought we were never going to be alone.' He tickled my ear as he kissed it.

Above and behind us was the sound of someone clearing his voice.

'Sssh,' I said.

'Excuse me, Blake, will you be needing breakfast?' It was Graham, the housekeeper.

As if neither of us would be hungry after snogging each other's faces off; had he never snogged? It makes you hungrier than hungry. It's because kissing burns up loads of calories. There's probably more point in going kissing than running a marathon, though, depressingly, ironing a shirt apparently burns double the calories of a snog but, since it's less than a tenth of the fun, it's not worth considering as an alternative exercise regime.

'Yes, we were just on our way,' Blake said, trying to sound serious. 'I was showing Lily the, um, curtains.'

'Yes, sir. They are fascinating.' Graham drawled his words ironically as if he could hardly be bothered to say them, and we heard him shuffle away.

A quick further snog, and we dashed into the dining room, giggling.

'Where's the food?' I asked, because there seemed to be none. When I found it – everything was in boxes or hiding under enormous silver covers – there was a ridiculous amount of it: eggs, bacon, sausages, tomatoes, mushrooms, toast, jams, cereal, fresh fruit and beautiful ruby red orange juice – my favourite.

'Don't hold back. Hungry?' Blake asked, laughing as I filled my plate, and then another.

'What? One's for Bea. I mean, it would be a shame for it to go to waste. Graham's such a great cook. That was a delicious dinner last night. I particularly enjoyed the lemon cheesecake with ginger biscuit crust. *Très magnifique!*' I said, kissing my fingers because it was really very good.

'I shall tell the chef! And nothing goes to waste with Poppy around – she's our walking-bin dog.'

'Poor Poppy. Dogs can get very ill eating a full fry up every morning,' I said, to show my sensible side and how concerned I can be for animal welfare. Then Bea walked in. 'Here's your nosh!' I said, holding a plate full of food out to her.

'Thanks. Hi, Blake.'

I swear Bea smiled at him.

'Did you sleep well, Bea? Hey, I like your T-shirt.'

'Oh thanks, it's vintage. I didn't hear a thing. I think Lily has ghosts in her imagination.' Bea giggled unconvincingly and batted her thick, Italian-style eyelashes. She was wearing a really tight T-shirt and drainpipes that showed her ridiculously long legs off. She could chop two inches off her legs and give them to me without noticing – that's how long they are.

'Well, at least I have an imagination,' I retorted.

'Now, girls! What are we going to do this morning? Do you want to look around the grounds?'

Both of us looked blankly back at Blake.

'I think we both know what the ground looks like, Blake,' I said, unimpressed. 'We do have ground in London, you know.'

'Not that kind of ground. Grounds, you know – stables, or the Chinese Garden, Victorian Greenhouse or the Magic Wood.'

'Wow! Could we do all of those things?' I asked because, although I wanted Blake to see me as a caring animal lover, I wanted to show an interest in his whole family heritage too. My legs may be short and my bum wide, but I am interested in history and would never insist that a multi-storey car park be built over Blakensold.

'And your dad's cars, can we see those?' Bea piped up.

'Sure, Dad would love that. Finish breakfast and put some trainers on. I just have to go and see Mum.'

'Do you think your mum would mind if I used the phone to call my mum? I should have done it last night, just to say we arrived.'

'Sure, there's one in the hallway by the stairs. See ya.' And off Blake disappeared, but not before he had winked at me.

At least, I hoped it was me he was winking at.

Calling All Mums

'Hey, Poppy.'

'Who is it? I'm very busy.'

'It's me! Lily. Remember you once had a sister?'

'Oh, you. Listen, Mum and Dad are going loco crazzee. What happened at the station?'

'Nothing, they just almost got arrested for causing a disturbance on the platform.'

'Dad's been sighted with the blonde again!'

'*Mon Dieu*. Can I speak to Mum?'

'She's furious. Do you really want to speak to her?'

'Maybe not. You can just tell her I'm safe in Norfolk.

She can call me on my mobile, if she wants.'

'OK. So how's your boyfriend?'

'Very rich and fabulously handsome, thank you.'

'Oh, so he's really boring then?'

'Just give Mum the message, Poppy.'

Poppy knew better than anyone else how to infuriate me, but I was so mature now, I knew that the best thing to do in the circumstance was to take a deep breath and slam the phone down, otherwise I'd just do something I'd regret.

'It wasn't Poppy by any chance?' asked Bea.

How could she always tell? While Bea used the phone to call her mum, I went to look out from the huge stone porch of the front door at the countryside spread out like a butter advert, all rich and pastoral. I felt quite cheery, and checked my texts.

Slum or palace? ghosts or dracula? Maya x
Ghost palace. L x

I texted back, but my smile was interrupted by a text from Poppy:

He must be really really boring then!

It was hard but I tried to rise above her childish behaviour and be grateful for staying in such a beautiful place, so unlike London and the city life I was used to. It is after all the differences in life that make it interesting.

I am so mature (and not like a piece of Cheddar, thank you!).

A Magical Mystery Tour

'I can't quite believe this place. Isn't it brilliant?' I smiled at Bea.

'What was that sneer about earlier at breakfast, Lily?'

'What sneer? Oh, just that you look too good in that T-shirt, and I wish it was mine, but it wouldn't look half as good on me.'

I am learning that it's not always good to show one's fleeting emotions with appropriate facial expressions – people don't like it. Mum doesn't. Dad hates it. Certainly teachers don't. Bea would make a good teacher.

'Oh, by the way, Mum said your mum's furious. She saw your dad walking down the King's Road. She's convinced he was going to that expensive underwear shop.'

Now it is all very well Poppy gossiping about our family, or me choosing to discuss it with Bea, but I don't necessarily want her to know about it before me.

'What? Marks & Spencer?'

'No, the posh women's one.'

'Well, I don't think they've made it illegal yet for old

men to go into ladies' underwear shops, though I think they should.'

'So what are you going to do?'

'About what?'

'Your dad and the underwear?'

'He's not wearing it, is he?' Nothing would have surprised me at that point.

'No! But at least we know it's not the office boy.'

'I'm not sure that's going to make Mum any happier. You know Bea, I don't really want to think about it.'

'Oh, OK. You're a bit touchy. So what are we going to do today? Just staying around here's going to be a bit boring.'

'It's our first day in the country, Bea. Look, it's beautiful. It'll be fun exploring.'

Bea just looked bored.

'OK, what do you want to do?'

'Can't we go into town to look at the shops?' asked Bea. 'I really want to go junking. It *is* Saturday. We could ask Lady B.'

Bea has a fascination with all things old. Old things and films mostly, but she likes to collect them, not just look at them. She spends most of her time training for that well-known sport of junking, which is digging up old things from jumble sales and charity shops. All of which can be fun when you've got nothing better to do, but I had to consider Blake.

'Yes, but Blake wants to show us around. We could go for a nice long walk.'

'If we must, but I'm going to ask Lady B if later —'

'You can't do that. She's got guests coming this afternoon. Don't you like the countryside? You're always going on about saving the earth. There's loads here.'

'Planet. Saving the planet, not the earth. Besides, I don't want to just hang out with you and Blake like some gooseberry, OK?'

I hoped it wasn't going to be a difficult day.

First Stop

We walked upstairs still bickering. I thought it would be fun to ask for a book to identify trees, birds and stuff. Bea thought I'd flipped. We brushed our teeth, our hair, changed our shoes and lip-glossed to perfection. We waited for Blake on the steps outside, flooded in sun, happy to have any opportunity to wear our sunglasses.

'So, girls,' he said, appearing with a knapsack, 'where do you want to go first? Shall we walk through the house down to the west wing?'

'Don't tell me – "My name is Blake and I am your guide for the day",' I said, trying to impersonate him, but I couldn't stop myself from laughing.

'You goon!' he said, laughing too.

'Surprise us,' said Bea flatly, looking the other way.

'OK, the magical mystery tour begins in the west wing. Ready?'

We trailed through the mausoleum of hereditary ancient collections of stuff on walls and wildlife stuffed in cases (quite a lot of stoats and weasels being attacked by owls, but no stuffed toads, I noticed).

'Do you like killing animals, Blake? Lots of taxidermy here,' said Bea in a not-exactly-friendly voice.

'I didn't kill them, Bea. I don't think about it. They've been there for hundreds of years.'

'Would you like to be shot and put in a glass case?' asked Bea.

'Oh look, what's that?' I asked as a diversion, pointing at something that might have been a badger or a very hairy ancestor.

We weaved through hallways to a Victorian plant house, crowded with rubber plants and palm trees, and completed by an indoor marble fountain of a cupid cherub aiming the arrow of love (had Blake bought me in here on purpose?) and tiny black and gold fish swimming madly between the lily pads. Everything was so old, exotic. It was strange to imagine this as a home. There were even clusters of green grapes trailing up the walls and hanging from the ceilings. Huge pots covered the mosaic-tiled floors, full of a zillion other exotic flowers and plants in every colour. It was hard to breathe the air – it was so wet and warm. It was like a mini Kew Gardens.

The Chinese Garden

It was a relief to hit the fresh air, as we made our way out of the glasshouse. We started to chat and walk across the gravel by the side of the house and round to a huge rhododendron bush. Blake was hacking at the under-growth with a stick and we had to hit back the leaves and branches to stop them from twanging into our faces.

As we pushed through into the other side, there was a clearing and a little pond with stepping stones crossing it.

'Ah, this is so cute. Is this the Chinese Garden?' I asked.

'Obviously not, Lily – it's a pond,' said Blake.

I shrugged and skipped across, the water lapping at my toes, glad I hadn't insisted on wearing my ballet pumps.

On the other side of the pond was a hedge with an *Alice in Wonderland* sized door cut into it. We squeezed through and walked around another obstructing hedge, and there inside the hedge walls was a small Chinese tea house being guarded by two real live peacocks. They were strutting and displaying their feathers magnificently and breaking the air with their calls for mates. In front of us was another pond, traversed by an arched, red wooden bridge, the end of which led inside the tea house. All about it were animals carved either from hedge, stone or wood, there was a stone rat coming out of the water that looked frighteningly real; out of the stump of an old tree, an ox seemed to be pulling a heavy load; a rabbit and a snake hid in the grass; a horse reared in the middle of a fountain, and a dragon sat on the top of the bridge. It was a Chinese wonderland.

'Wow,' I said, sitting down on a bamboo bench. 'This is amazing.'

'Dad had it built for Mum when they got married because they'd met backpacking around China or something,' explained Blake

'That's so romantic. Isn't it weird thinking of our parents as being smoochy backpackers?' I said.

'Yuck. Whatever, it's disgusting. The animals are all supposed to represent the different parts of the Chinese horoscope, all living in harmony together. Do you know what sign you are?' Blake asked me. 'I'm a horse. You better not be a rat.'

'Rat? *Je ne sais pas.* But I love it here,' I said, beginning to relax into the seat.

'*Allez oop,* Lily. *On y va,*' said Blake.

'Trying to impress me with your schoolboy French, eh? *Très bien, monsieur, très mal.*'

'No, actually, we always say it when we go hunting.'

'"*En hiver?*" Doesn't that mean "In winter"? You say that when you go hunting?'

'You hunt?' Bea's eyes stood out on little stalks. 'So you do like killing animals!'

'Sometimes. But not any more,' countered Blake.

'Oh good, because you know it's actually illegal?' added Bea. 'Those poor little foxes.'

'Poor little foxes, my bum. You clearly haven't seen a chicken coop ravaged by a fox, have you? It slaughters or injures them all and only takes one. Now that's savage. Remember, you're in the country – we're overrun by foxes here.'

'So are we in London. I saw one walking down the steps of St Paul's one night. I still wonder if it had been to church,' I said, not wanting any argument of the Countryside Alliance to break out.

'Been through the bins more like. Lily, do you really think that the fox had been in confession or something?' asked Bea, tetchily.

'It might. Foxes must pray when they're hunted.'

'Blake's right: you are crazy.'

'I am not.'

'No, she's not,' agreed Blake. 'Lily is perfect. Perfectly craz—, I mean unique.'

'They only made one of me,' I told them. 'And there are good reasons for that.'

'But, Lily, they only made one of all of us,' said Blake, confused.

'And I'm sure God had good reason to do that too. Imagine two Blakes . . . which would I kiss?'

Blake blushed a beautiful shade of beetroot. As I looked at him, all I could hear was Bea making vomiting noises. What was she doing, trying to destroy the moment? But at least I'd stopped the argument.

Magical Wood

We were walking out of one secret world, through and down into a wood. I was about to ask if this was the magic wood, but realised I might break the spell if it was. Surely the whole point of being in the countryside was the unravelling and the looking and watching as one piece of nature turned into another.

The wood was shadow cold. Ice-green moss slipped over the tree trunks and down into a carpet of earth, sticks, leaves, and ivy. The birdsong was more muted than in the Chinese Garden and, between the crunch of breaking twigs underfoot, you could hear the scurrying of busy creatures. Wild Wooders?

'I wouldn't like to be here at night,' whispered Bea.

'Nor would I,' I added for solidarity.

'Well, if you behave yourselves, I won't leave you here.'

Blake was so reassuring.

A big old oak tree signalled a path that turned steeply downhill. Bea and I held on to each other as we scuttled on the backs of our heels down the dell and after Blake.

I saw great shafts of light falling through the tall trees, sunlight dancing amongst the leaves and their branches, the dust in the air swirling magically like a million little Tinkerbells.

'Wow, it's wonderful. I love it. Bea, it's an enchanted forest.'

'Wow!' she said, but I could sense the sarcasm.

'I knew you'd like it,' said Blake.

It *was* magic. Blake and I sat down on a log, very close to each other, and his hand was holding mine behind my back.

'It feels very fecund here, doesn't it?' said Bea, standing and looking at us.

'Pardon, Bea?'

'Fecund. Do I have to be a dictionary? It means fertile.'

'What, like there's something in the air, eh eh?'

'No! God, you're sex mad, Lily.'

'But I never mentioned sex,' I protested.

And, of course, at the mere mention of sex, Blake and I were snorting laughter through our noses whilst holding our hands over our mouths, laughing out our embarrassment.

'Honestly, you two!' Bea stormed off in a strop, annoyance rumbling in the air as she strode away.

'Oh no!' said Blake.

'Trouble in paradise I fear. I better make sure she's all right.'

'Wait, Lily, kiss me first.'

I couldn't say no. Bea was right – the wood must have been fecund. Blake was definitely growing on me.

CHAPTER FIVE

Just The Two Of Us

Escaping Bea

'Just look at all these DVDs – there must be one you want to watch. Or what about the swimming pool? You could go for a lovely swim in the heated pool or read a book. Oh please, Bea. Pretty please?'

We were in Blake's room at the top of the house and he had more DVDs than you can find to rent in a Blockbuster's. He also had a library of games, CDs and a fridge stacked like a hotel minibar (without alcohol), and a real popcorn-making machine.

'That will be great fun – alone!' she said sulkily.

'It won't be that bad. You can make popcorn, drink ginger beer and play some computer games. I just need a little time, like an hour or two, alone with Blake. It's just that I really need to talk to him, to find out if I properly like him.'

'You mean snog him more like. Well, you should have thought about all that before inviting me here. Honestly, Lily, we haven't done one thing I want to do.'

I was feeling a little ashamed that my plan was so transparent, but I was sticking to it.

'I know what I said and I'm sorry. Look, we've got loads of days here and we'll do lots of other things together. We haven't been riding yet and Blake's got a quad bike.'

Bea looked distinctly bored with the idea of a quad bike or anything else that Blake might or might not have.

'Look, I promise I'll speak to Lady B about going into town. How's that?'

'When?'

Have you ever felt like you are pushing the largest elephant in the world, uphill, and it was threatening to collapse on your head?

The day in the woods, Blake and I had had two beautiful snogging moments, and the rest of the day had been taken up trying to make Bea feel like the most important one amongst us – in other words, less left out. We'd eaten the contents of Blake's knapsack – a special packed lunch of peanut butter and Nutella sandwiches – when we were rowing in a boat on the lake. A sudden downpour of rain had soaked us to the bone, as we tried to row to land, and were forced indoors. There we'd played backgammon and Monopoly and even let her win. We let her choose what CDs we'd listen to and DVDs we'd watch, but nothing seemed to stop her bottom lip protruding like a spoiled baby. I'm not sure she knew what she wanted, but I was pretty sure it wasn't anything we could give her.

'We'll be back asap. Promise,' I said, with as much enthusiasm as I could muster.

'OK. So when will that be?'

'At lunchtime. We're only going for a short bike ride down to the river and back, I think.'

'OK.' Bea huffed. 'I'll probably watch a movie. See you later.' She wrinkled her nose up at me, when she said goodbye. I left her in the nursery and flew down the stairs to find Blake.

'Yeeha! Let's go!' I planned to say, but when I saw him turn around I felt strangely shy. He smiled at me and I could feel my stomach salsa-dance into my throat and then turn around to tango, colliding with my heart; just saying a simple hi ended up being hard enough. What was doing this to me?

'Where's Bea?' he asked.

'I left her in your room watching telly. I thought we could, well, you said last night that you wanted to do something by ourselves,' I said, staring at my feet. And then it was as if I'd never looked at my feet before. I was sure they weren't always that huge.

'Well, well done, Lily. You mean we're free for the day?'

'Almost – just the morning. Where are the bikes you were talking about? We could go for a ride.'

I was keen to try the quad bikes. I fancied myself as a bit of an action girl, *Charlie's Angels* style. They couldn't be that difficult to handle.

'What are you thinking of, Lily?' he said, as if what I had suggested wasn't the most innocent thing in the world.

'What? Nothing, why? What are you thinking of?'

He did one of his weird, raised eyebrow things. 'I'll tell you when we get there. I'm going to teach you something interesting. Come on.'

Sacré bleu! I thought. What if he started teaching me his advanced kissing technique – would that be as interesting as quad bike riding?

What If The Brakes Don't Work?

'Good job you've got jeans on,' Blake said to me.

'Of course I've got jeans on. I'm not going to walk around half-naked in my knickers, am I?' I asked, as we made our way outside.

'I meant instead of shorts, duh!' He smiled, as we walked towards the garage where the cars were kept. For most people that would simply mean walking a short distance, but, since the whole of Blake's house was spread out like a box of Lego spilled across the grass, everything took about ten minutes to walk to.

One garage was scattered with pieces of an old car, but in the back there were a couple of ancient black bikes in a corner. Blake gave me the lady's one.

'Do you expect me to ride this?'

'Of course. It was my granny's, and if it was good enough for her . . . and it still works.'

'But I thought we were going to . . .'

'What?'

'It doesn't matter,' I said, because it didn't, and I didn't want him to think I was no fun.

I had to sit up straight on top of a hard saddle with wide, thin wheels and a basket, and it weighed a ton. Nothing like my mountain bike back home, and the brakes both squeaked, as if mice were trapped inside them.

The sky had lost all its Indian summer feel. Even the air smelled more like autumn – it had that cold country dampness after night-time rain, when, as the day gets warmer and the earth gently heats up, you can smell everything as if it was all freshly made, almost as exciting as an unburned apple crumble coming warm out of the oven (unburned is quite a rarity at our home) or newly baked cookies.

We cycled down past the lake, which had a thin mist rising up from it.

'Watch out for the sheep. They don't like being run over,' Blake shouted over his shoulder, just as a flock of geese skirted around him, forcing him to brake.

'Ha ha!' I laughed back, enjoying the ride. Not having to avoid cars or people made everything wide open and completely different from London. Especially with Blake there.

We freewheeled down a small hill and then out of the back estate gate and on to a proper country road, but there wasn't any traffic and you could see the stretch of fields, only broken by the red brick of houses.

'Blake, where are we going?' I asked.

'This way. Just follow me.'

'So you do know where you're going?'

'Oh yes, and I know where you're going too,' he said, turning and winking back at me, and a little shiver of a smile spread over my face and down into my toes.

How is it when other boys wink at me I just think they look dumb, but when Blake does, it seems funny, clever, lovably ironic and sophisticated – all the very things I want to be.

Trusting Boys

It was a good job that I trusted Blake, or else I would have felt a little like I was being led down a country road to nowheresville – fast. And I was just about to compose a letter to the universe – you know, one of those, *Dear Universe, Please look after me and make sure that I'm not cycling alongside a mass-murderer* type things (not that he could have really been a mass-murderer, because if he'd been going to do it, I'd have already been dead). This reminded me, in the way that thoughts do, that I'd better ring Mum when I got back, because she hadn't rung me and she might like to know that I hadn't been murdered. I knew I had told Poppy, but that's not exactly the most reliable way of passing on a message. I was also a little curious to know what exactly was happening with Dad. You see, you can't take your eye off the button, or whatever it is, for a moment, not with Dad around. Things have a tendency of happening just when you aren't looking, or, as my gran used to say, you have to keep your eyes peeled and on the ball. How very uncomfortable.

So I was thinking all these incredibly important life and death philosophical thoughts, whilst singing sunshiney songs perfect for cycling, when I was rudely interrupted by a shout. This was a bit like having your iPod headphones pulled sharply out of your ears by your dad.

'STOP! Stop, Lily! Are you not listening to me at all?' yelled Blake.

Apparently not. I screeched to a halt and had to cycle all the way back to him.

'Obviously it wasn't interesting enough to listen to,' I told him.

'Ha ha. You could be a comedienne if someone taught you some jokes. We were supposed to stop twenty metres back, but you've got to keep quiet.'

'Why?' I whispered.

'Because we're climbing over the wall.'

'Oh. OK. Why?'

I soon saw it was pointless to try and get anything sensible out of him (he kept shushing me and rolling his eyes), so I followed him back up the road and he chained our bikes to a handy tree.

'Stay there, I've got to look out for the farmer.'

Why? Were we going to see the farmer for lunch, and if so, why were we climbing over his wall and not going through a door? Maybe we were going to steal more sheep for Blakensold, I thought, but how could they fit any more in?

The Great Apple War

Blake hauled himself over the top of the wall.

He kept his head down and then he reached for my

hands, to try and pull me up. Useless. I was more likely to pull him off. So he had to jump back down and give me a leg up, which ended with quite a lot of bum pushing, much to my serious embarrassment. It wouldn't have been so bad if I didn't like him so much. No, that sounds bad, as if I'd want a stranger pushing my bum up a wall, which, of course, I wouldn't – what do you take me for?!

Finally I made it on top of the wall and for a moment I just sat and looked at this beautiful orchard full of trees covered in red and green apples.

'Jump,' hissed Blake.

When Blake asks me to jump, I jump, and did so after him into the long thick grass.

'It's my favourite orchard,' he told me, reaching for my hand. 'I always used to come here with my brother when we were small. I just knew you'd like it. It's amazing when it's covered in blossom.'

'But it isn't.'

'Of course not – wrong time of year. But isn't it beautiful?'

'Beautiful?' Most of the boys I know don't describe things as being beautiful. If they mean it, they're usually talking about a girl, and then they say 'fit' or 'well buff', which is very different, but I don't think either phrase could describe an orchard full of apples.

The wind blew the branches, and the overripe apples

swung and fell, crashing and jumping to the ground.

We walked about, dodging the windfalls and collecting the unbruised apples for my pockets. The worm infested ones I showed to Blake with a mixture of horror and disgust, until he threw one at me, and war was declared – The Great Apple War.

When the rain started, it was the peculiar fat drops I like to open my mouth and drink in, until I think of Bea telling me all about global warming and all the gunk put into the atmosphere by planes, which rather puts me off. Sometimes the idea is nicer than the reality, like when Bea told me about how they make strawberry milkshakes that have no milk and no strawberries in them – just seven hundred chemicals!

'Don't you love the rain?' I said, because the air was warm and the rain was soft when it started. But it soon started to pelt it down.

'Quick, let's go shelter in the barn,' Blake said, and pointed in front of us. There was a barn full of hay bales and, as if the rain wasn't enough of a reason, the man upstairs (otherwise known as God) thoughtfully provided some thunder and lightning.

If there is one thing I don't like, apart from:

1) Bulls charging at me in an open field;
2) Dad shouting at me first thing in the morning;
3) Baby Bay sitting on me with a smelly naked bum;

4) Mum burning dinner or talking to my teachers at
   school,

it's raw lightning – especially when I'm near a tree. I
didn't need anything else to help me run the one-minute
mile into the barn.

So all at once Blake and I were in the barn together,
shaking our hair dry like dogs – Blake, like a recently
trimmed terrier, just had to brush it over with his hand; I
supposed I looked more like a soaking, long haired, Old
English sheepdog.

I'd never been in a barn before. It was damned good
fun. You can jump from one bale to another and fall off
to play dead, and not even hurt yourself, and though it's
a little itchy and scratchy, it's not so bad when you've got
Blake to kiss the scratches better.

'Ah, poor little Lily,' he said and kissed me better.

I don't know which bit I prefer the most about kissing:

1) Before it happens, quaking with all the excitement?

2) Whilst it's happening, when you're lost in a long, dark,
warm, soft tunnel and you're wishing there isn't a light at the
end of it? or

3) Afterwards, post kiss, when you can think about it,
again and again – dissecting each and every part and particle,
but oh so much more slowly, later in your mind?

Is it possible to become addicted to kissing? I think I
might be.

I don't know if we had been kissing for an hour, a year, a day or a minute. That is the whole point of time. How can you ever measure time when it is so easily lost. You can't hold it, or tame it; it comes and goes as quick as it likes and it has no loyalty to anyone, certainly not to me.

Outside the rain and thunder tirelessly roared, but we were cosy and dry, and I was very happy, engulfed by the smell of straw and warm next to Blake.

'Isn't kissing the best thing?' Blake said, as he came up for air.

'It all depends who you're kissing,' I murmured, to make sure that he understood that kissing me was *très spécial et ne pas drôle!*

'What? So are you like some kind of expert? Have you kissed loads of boys, Lily?' He looked a little upset at the prospect, but not as upset as I felt for appearing like some cheap sket.

'No, of course I haven't.'

I wondered if this was the point where I had to tell him that I had in fact kissed William, his friend at camp, moments before I had first kissed him. I was trying to believe that William's kiss didn't really count, since his mouth had encased both my nose and mouth; it was more like something you learn for pool-side resuscitation training.

All the same, I didn't want to appear naive. It is very

difficult getting that balance right, I find, especially when white lies are involved. This is what is called a dichotomy (my favourite English word) – a separation into two divisions that differ widely from each other. I always think it sounds like more of a pudding or an operation really, and that is a dichotomy in itself.

'No, what I meant was that it's got to be nicer kissing you than kissing a sheep or something,' I explained.

'That is so kind of you, Lily.'

'Don't mention it.'

'Well, I'm sure you're right; kissing you would only be slightly nicer than kissing a cowpat.'

'Kissed many cowpats recently?' I asked.

'No, but maybe I should just try a few more kisses with you to make sure you're human and not . . .'

'Vegetable!' I screamed, predictably.

'No . . . a cowpat!'

He must have seen the look in my eyes, because he jumped up and backed away from me, saying, 'I was only joking, really I was. Put the apples down. No, Lily you don't want to do that, honestly you don't. Please?'

But it was too late and I was having too much fun. I pelted the apples around the barn, chasing him over the huge stacks of bales. Occasionally a cry of, 'Ow! That hurt,' came from him. Then he tried to shoot them back at me.

At some point the rain stopped, and the lightning eased out of the sky and back up to wherever it came from. I had stopped laughing and crowing for a moment to get my breath as he hid, and that's when I heard the voices.

'Those bloody kids have been in the orchard again. I'm telling you, Patrick, we're going to have to put up electric wire. I'm going to teach them a lesson.'

Blake's head appeared above a hay bale with his finger to his mouth to signal silence (as if I was about to have a chat!) and he pointed towards the door. We quietly picked up the mushed-up apples as quickly as we could and hid in the shadows, waiting for the footsteps to either come in to find us or to fade away.

I prayed my very hardest, apologised from the bottom of my heart and promised, once again, to never ever do anything that wasn't kind and good. My previous prayers seemed just a rehearsal – after all, wasn't it legal for farmers to shoot trespassers? And what a stupid idea of Blake's to make me have so much fun doing something illegal. What if a farmer saw me and shot me? Mum would never allow me to go away again. And what would we say to Blake's parents? This was more terrifying than the idea of being shot.

At least if I *was* shot, the grown-ups would feel sorry for me and probably bring me presents in hospital. I was wondering just how much being shot would hurt, when the sound of voices became muffled by the noise of a tractor's engine which drowned everything out. As it faded away, I felt Blake's hand grasp mine and I opened my eyes to look at him.

'Sorry,' he whispered. 'We'd better get out of here.'

I nodded my head enthusiastically. Inside my brain I was already climbing the wall and riding up the lane. And that's just when I felt my phone vibrate the arrival of a message:

Hope you having loads of fun. Will call tonight.
love you, Mum x Bay x

CHAPTER SIX

As Cross As A Wasp, As Mad As A Bea

Parents Are Different

Blake and I ran up the lane with the heaviest bikes in the world. Freewheeling down, it had seemed like only a couple of metres, but going up was more like a couple of kilometres, with two flat tyres each – courtesy of the farmer – and of course it started to rain again, but with the shouts of farmers behind us what else could we do?

Blake suggested a short cut across a field.

'But, Blake,' I pleaded, 'can't you ring your mum and ask her to collect us? Please? You can use my mobile.'

He looked at me and shook his head. 'I can't, Lily, my mum's not like that. She'd just go ballistic. I'd more likely ring Graham in an emergency. Are you sure you can't make it home?'

'I could ring *my* mum.'

'But she's in London.'

'But that's what mums are for – to get you out of sticky situations, to make things easier when life is hard, to make you laugh when you're really upset.'

'Doesn't sound remotely like my mother.'

Blake was full of apologies, but it was me who felt sorry for him. What was the point of having all this money and stuff if you couldn't ask your mum for help?

He had already told me the cautionary tale of his brother who had been sent off to work on a cousin's sheep farm in the middle of the outback in Australia, for the whole of his summer holidays, after Lord B had found him and his friends drunk in their wine cellar, having opened all the vintage champagne. Unfortunately it didn't have quite the effect it was supposed to: his brother didn't want to return to England – he liked Australia!

I was just thinking all this, when I spectacularly slipped into a cowpat. Blake's reaction? He laughed. Suddenly, the thought of Blake being sent to Australia was strangely appealing. Whether he liked it or not, I might.

In The Diary Doghouse — Woof!

Dear Diary,

I am writing this while soaking in the bath. I am in the bath to escape Bea's fury, and Blake, who I'm furious with. I am furious at Blake because I don't like being covered in an interesting mix of straw, rotten apple, mud, cowpat and shame.

I had to escape Bea's 'poor me' moans, and Lady B's guilt-making stares — made worse by her telling me, 'I'm not saying it's your fault, Lily, but you really should learn not to be so easily led at your age. I can't understand why you would leave your best friend behind. Of course, it's all Blake's fault, because you two are the guests and he is older than you, if only just and nadynadynadyblah bla noooooooooargh!' (Is that translatable into French, or have I invented a new international language?)

The farmer had called Blake's parents. With no other kids around, and with his brother and his reputation, Blake was the obvious suspect. I know we trespassed, but anybody would think we'd invented the atom bomb and pressed the button!

I don't care if I shrivel up like a prune in the bath. I'd rather be a dried apricot than have to sit at dinner being cross-examined or stared at like a blue-bottomed baboon.

I wish I was at home. At least then I'd only have the trauma of family rows to face, not my own disgrace in the land of the rich and posh.

Think Maya was v. sensible <u>not</u> coming. Who wants to be in the boring country anyway? I know Maya is quite a witch, but I *wonder if she foresaw all of this disaster in a crystal ball? I wouldn't be surprised.*

Praying Lady B hasn't called Mum. Think I should call Mum, though what if Dad answers the phone? Not sure I want to speak to him. I might ask about the blonde.

Zut alors! C'était bon pendant que ça durait.

Roughly translates as: It was good while it lasted.

Wonder what they will write about me in the newspapers . . . 'A sorely missed child; a brilliant talent, tragically ended, after her father strangled her for showing him up in front of some VIPP – very important posh people.'

Whilst Mum will probably make me wash up for the rest of my life. Can you die from too much washing up?

Who cares what happens at dinner – Je m'en fiche: *I'm already dead, or as good as.* Cela m'est égal, *as Marie Antoinette probably said before her head was guillotined off. 'I don't care' is so much more believable than, 'Let them eat cake'. Who'd be hungry at a time like that? Besides, I'll probably never eat again.*

My end is nigh . . .

Lily Lovitt était ici, sur la terre, *once upon a time.*

'Lily?'

I knew it was Bea knocking. Even her door-knocking was distinctive. And irritating!

'What?'

'Can I come in?'

'I'm not dressed.'

'I know – you're in the bath. Lily, let me in. I promise I won't look! It's not like I haven't witnessed your nudey scenes a million times.'

'What nudey scenes? I'm hardly Paris Hilton!'

Whatever I said made no difference to Bea. She marched in and stood there, arms akimbo, to show off what she was wearing, like a blooming butterfly. She then started to do a little dance, like nothing had happened, because she was wearing this beautiful gold dress.

Had I been forgiven?

'So do you like it? Lady B gave me this dress because she said I needed something to make me feel special, after being deserted and then starved by you and evil Blake.'

The word 'smug' had never had such meaning for me before. If smug was a new car, Bea's face could have been the advert. I must look it up in French, it's sure to be a good word.

'You! Starved? Hardly!' I retaliated. 'You had three ginger beers, two chocolate bars, a tub of popcorn and a bag of nuts and raisins, whilst lying down watching *Pirates of the Caribbean*. We had a couple of bruised apples, and had to walk uphill for two miles, pushing bikes that weighed a ton with flat tyres through a field of cow poo.'

'Well, you should have thought of that.'

She always said things like that, but this time it was in such a nasty tone, I found myself sneering beneath my beard of bubbles. Bea couldn't stop herself swirling around the bathroom in her web of smugness. After a bit she seemed more like a moth or a mosquito than a butterfly, and one I wanted to swat.

'Why are you pulling a face, Lily?' she asked, when she stopped twirling for a moment. 'It's quite ugly, and if the wind changes you might stay like that for ever. It's dinner in ten minutes, so hadn't you better get out of the bath? You know we're eating with a really famous fashion designer tonight. What are you going to wear?'

I could have sworn that there was a gloat, as large as the iceberg that sank the Titanic, floating in her voice.

What To Wear? That Is The Question!

It was a good question: what *was* I going to wear? I had nothing to compete with an original 1960s Chanel mini-dress creation, made out of tiny gold and silver metal discs on a background of gold silk. Bea looked incredible, and she certainly didn't look thirteen. It's amazing what make-up can do, and those legs. Why did God give the giraffe's to her, and the pit pony variety to me? Was it because of something I had done in another life? Something my father had done in this one?

'Well, Bea, going through my choices of poo-stinking

jeans and my old shredded jeans, cutting a hole in a towel and wearing it as a mini-dress poncho might be the best option.'

She raised her eyes at me the way my mum does, turned and left. At least it let me get out of the bath, just as my phone began to ring. I ran into the bedroom and grabbed it.

'Hello, the misery line,' I said with meaning, dripping over the carpet with one arm keeping a towel in place.

'Do you want me to wait for you?' Bea interrupted, loitering by the door.

'No, no need. I'll be right down.'

'Good, because I was going to say I don't like being rude to Lady B, after she's been so kind to me.' And off Bea trotted like a giddy show pony – less teacher's pet, more adults' favourite.

Of course I was jealous. Embarrassed and jealous. I felt like a prime idiot. *Un imbécile parfait*, about summed it up. *I* was meant to be impressing Lady B.

'Sweetie, it's Mum. What's up? How's it going?'

'It's horrible and I hate it. They're all posh and laughing at me.'

'What? Surely not Bea?'

'She's the worst. Has Lady B called you?'

'No, about what?'

OK, deep breath hold it together. Say enough of the truth

to get her sympathy, but not enough to make her angry.

'Well, it was Blake who wanted me to go on a bike ride with him and Bea was annoyed, because she felt like a gooseberry and stayed behind. Then Blake said I should climb over a wall and it was into an orchard. But I didn't know he didn't own it: they own everything else around here for miles. And then we got chased by the farmers and I'm in disgrace with Lady B, his mum, for letting Blake tell me what to do. And, and Mum, there's this posh dinner tonight and Blake's mum has given Bea this really amazing designer vintage dress to wear for dinner and I've got nothing to wear, and I wish I could just come home. I hate it here.'

I was telling such a good tale, I'd practically made myself cry.

'Oh darling, you poor little Lilypops,' Mum said, but I wasn't convinced from her tone that she totally believed me.

'I know, Mum. It's not fair.'

'Well, lucky then that I put your premiere dress into your bag when you weren't looking. I thought something special might happen.'

'You didn't? Where?' I was running around the room trying to find my bag. Why hadn't I seen it when I'd unpacked?

'It's in the side pocket. It might be a bit creased but, hey, it's meant to be, isn't it? The Crecian Grecian look?'

I found it just as the dinner gong rang.

'Mum, you are brilliant. I'm sorry I haven't asked you anything about home, but I've got to get dressed and rush down for dinner. Mum, you're the best, official. Love you.'

'Don't worry, Lily, I'll call tomorrow. Have fun tonight.'

With my premiere dress and high-heeled espadrilles, I knew I wouldn't look like a million dollars but I might, with some lip-gloss and mascara, make it up to a twenty.

Quel choix possible? It was the best I could do, but I was not looking forward to the showdown at supper.

Love Knots

It is odd the way love can so easily have its head turned about by a dollop of discomfort, like how I felt towards Bea and Blake. Poor Blake. Adults are so strange, but at least I knew I could always ring my mum if the worst happened. I couldn't imagine what it must be like, not to have anyone to tell when things go bad or stuff happens, which it has a habit of doing.

My stomach might have felt bad, knotted by Blake and the love and hate all mixed up, but walking down those stairs alone to the drawing room for pre-dinner drinks, or cocktails as they called them, I felt scared, small, silly and out of my depth. I ran back up to the room and called Mum. Not to tell her and blub, I just needed to hear her voice again. It went straight to answerphone.

I didn't leave a message.

Scrubs Up Nicely

'Lily.'

I looked up from halfway down the staircase on my second time down, and there was Blake running towards me. The same Blake I wanted to be sent to Australia. Then he smiled, and a glow of warmth spread through me like melting butter on toast and I seemed to go all floppy inside. He looked so strange dressed in a suit, that for a moment I didn't recognise him, and I wanted to laugh or cry, probably both with a handstand in between, but it would have been a bit difficult on the stairs, and a little rude in this dress.

'You look fantastic,' we both said together, holding each other's arms. I kissed his cheek, he rubbed it and asked if there were any lip-gloss marks. Boys these days, eh!

Suddenly walking in with Blake to that scary place full of grown-ups, I didn't care. I didn't care about the silence as we entered the room or when Lord B said, 'I see the two reprobates have kindly agreed to join us. Ha!' Whatever that meant.

'Come on, Dickie,' said Lady B. 'I said I'd dealt with it. There are to be no recriminations, all right? The business is finished. Now would you two like some of Graham's delicious homemade lemonade? Come and say hello to our guests.'

The guests, Mr and Mrs La Real, were Spanish and a bit like people from a glossy fashion magazine but right there in front of you. The man was wearing scary high-heeled cowboy boots with coloured diamonds all over them. Very odd! His wife was all gold and jewels. There were also three other people but I couldn't remember any of their names because I was so busy being polite, smiling, saying hello, as well as being fabulously charming that it was hard to remember them. All except one woman wearing a man's pinstripe trouser suit, who called everyone 'darling', growled with laughter, stank of perfume, smoked a cigar and I could've sworn was wearing a dead cat on her head, but it might have been her hair. She reminded me of Cruella de Ville from *One Hundred and One Dalmatians*. She was a very famous artist. I know because she told me.

Bea smiled at me, in a nice way, as if she knew nothing more was going to happen to embarrass me. In fact the whole night would have been fine, if not for Hubert.

Flip Like A Salmon

Who on earth calls their child Hubert anyway! Spanish designers, apparently. The poor boy – his whole name was Hubert La Real (the royal!). You had to feel sorry for him – aside from his bizarre behaviour, he also had a silly way of saying the most basic things; he made my baby brother Bay look mature, and Bay is two, whilst Hubert is apparently thirteen. And the worst thing was that Blake couldn't see how stupid and arrogant he was, because, after all, they were old friends, and so I just had to smile.

The problem was not just that he was prime-time material – 'I can't eat this; I have to sit there; I'm allergic to everything' – but that he was really good-looking, too. At least he *was* good-looking, you might think, but no, it was bad, because his looks made Bea's heart flip like a salmon.

'Lily, have you *seen* him?' She excitedly dashed over to me, gripping my arm, whispering in my ear, irritation gone not because of forgiveness, but because of Hubert.

'Who?'

'He's called Hubert La Real, and I'm in love.'

'Hubert UnReal more like.'

'Look at him. He's like Johnny Depp but not as old.'

He did look like him, but you just had to speak to the boy to realise that even a film star wouldn't be as rude as he was.

Throughout dinner, the four of us sat at the bottom of the table, the grown-ups at the top, drinking their way through bottle after bottle of wine. They should have just got some wine boxes like my mum does. I wasn't sure what was worse: talking to Lord B, Toad of Toad Hall, or talking to the La Reals' son, Hubert. I mean what are you supposed to say when someone says, 'Last week I went shark hunting with my uncle. We killed two sharks. It was fantastic.' Apart from, 'Butcher!'

Which was what I thought Bea would reply. Instead she just glazed over like a honey-baked ham with a perma-smile and said, 'Wow, Hubert, what was it like? It must have been amazing. You are so brave.'

What became of her Save the Mammals of the Global Ocean Campaign membership?

'I told you already. It was fantastic. It was OK. OK?'

Then, rather rudely, Hubert turned his back on poor Bea and talked about boring PlayStation and Xbox games to Blake. Every now and again, Bea would try to join in.

In normal circumstances this could have been fine, if only her eyeballs weren't magnetically attached to his face. Every movement he made, her eyes followed, like a heat-seeking missile, or a magnet with iron filings – it was seriously scary.

Some girls are obviously better at being in love than

others. I mean it's not like I'd ever behave like a total idiot! Poor Bea, she couldn't see what she looked like or sounded like, but I could and so could everyone else. Poor, poor Bea. Obviously I wanted her to be in love, but not with such a jerk; she deserved better. Much better.

Luckily I had the grown-ups to look at for entertainment. Hubert's mother was hilarious – shrieking and cackling; at one point she even started to sing. At least my mother knows not to sing in front of me – even she'd be embarrassed by that. For a millisecond I had a little sympathy for Hubert, until he turned around and sneered at me. *Très charmant!*

Tortured Zombies

Dear Diary,
Hurray! Not dead. All that fear for nothing, wasted.

Dinner was not wasted on me. Was delicious. Artichokes, which are great because not only is there lots of tearing off and dipping and nibbling but they always make my pee smell really peculiar, like instant chemistry. Asparagus does it too, and if you eat beetroot your pee goes pink, yet blueberries do nothing. Curious.

Then there was lamb with creamy potatoes and, best of all, hot chocolate mousse cake with vanilla ice cream. YUM. Then grapes and cheese. I finished it all. Amazing, since I was feeling so sick I was never going to eat again. I remembered to use the correct knives this time. I'm about ready to dine with the Queen, practically. Lady B told us all – Bea, Blake, Hubert (yuck) and me – to go up and watch a film in the nursery, as they wanted to have 'grown-up chats'. I was a little worried. Well, I know what grown-up chats mean; at home, it's when adults drink all the wine boxes in the house, get really, really drunk and then shout very loudly at each other. And if that was going to happen between Lord and Lady B, let alone the woman dressed like a man (the man/woman), I was happy to disappear into another part of the house and escape Hubert's amazing singing mother – Mum's not half as embarrassing. Love Mum. I've almost completely forgotten about her horrid last boyfriend – FishMan. Poor Mum, and The Blonde and Dad. Quelle mess.

Once upstairs, Hubert wanted to play PlayStation on the giant screen and nobody said, no let's watch a film.

Bea said that, if Hubert wanted to play, she wanted to watch him shoot. And Blake said he'd play Hubert. Honestly! Wonder if Bea thought she was giving me a taste of my own medicine? I prefer being alone to watching PlayStation games.

Pour l'amour de Dieu!

Then a message bleeped on my phone. It was from Maya.

Wats up kookachoo? Still mates? M x
Stuck in nightmare. Wish you were here. L x
E-mail 2moz. At boring party prem now, 2
    noisy. wish you were here. M x
Me 2. L x

Ah, love that Maya. Am I being disloyal saying that? Bea is the one who is up here in Norfolk. Anyway, shouldn't Maya be in Hawaii by now?

Am in bed now, alone. Cassandra in I Capture the Castle *did a lot of that, in the castle; alone, writing. Maybe it's because I'm a writer? (Je suis un auteur, I will say when I live in Paris to anybody who asks.) Am I so odd I simply can't watch PlayStation? Am quite snoozy. Have decided to call the painting on our wall Mrs Snoopy, not that she looks like the dog (BUT maybe she does), but because she always seems to be snooping at whatever I'm up to. I'm not scared of her; I'm not ever going to be scared again. I am Lily the Fearless. Wish I didn't need to go to the loo so badly – the bed's so cosy and warm. The lights in the bathroom are out. Someone is stumbling about the corridor, what if it's the man/woman? Maybe I could go to sleep and forget about the loo? But what if I wet the bed?* Mon Dieu! *Wish Bea would come back. Will I ever make it home alive?*

'There you are? Why did you go off like that?'

Bea was sitting in bed when I got back from the loo.

'You were the one who went off sidling up with Monsieur La Royale indeed. Since when have you liked watching PlayStation?'

'Always. It's fun,' she said simply.

'Fun? And what about the shark thing? I thought you protected beasts of the ocean?'

'I'm tired. I don't want to talk about it,' Bea said,

snuggling down in the bed.

'Fine! Give me back my pillow,' I demanded.

'Why do you have to be such a baby?'

'Why do *you* have to be such a baby?'

'Oh, shut up.'

'No, *you* shut up,' I said, determinedly. I made faces into the darkness. 'Baby indeed!' I seethed until sleep pulled me into a series angry, battling dreams.

If you are thinking of going on holiday with a best friend, some friendly advice – think again.

CHAPTER SEVEN

Why, Oh Why?

Dreaming Or Mad

'And those are just some of the reasons why it's no surprise we've never been on holiday before, because this is the way you are, Miss Lily Lovitt!' Bea woke me up early as she was practising a little speech in the bathroom mirror.

For a moment I thought I was still dreaming. Dreaming or mad. I wondered what else she'd said before I'd woken up. I sat up in bed and coughed loudly.

I said, 'Sorry, Bea, were you talking to me, or someone else?'

She came and stood by the bed. 'I haven't said anything I wouldn't say to your face.'

'Like?'

'Your moods are impossible to keep up with, Lily. I don't know what's going to upset you next.'

'Oh, and you don't have moods? You can't even be by yourself for an hour.'

'And all *you* try to do is manipulate everyone around you.'

'Oh, Miss Perfect Bea. It must be great being you in your perfect home, with your perfect family, perfect American holidays, with your perfect legs.'

'Shut up! Just because you come from a family of freaks! Look at your mum!'

'What about my mum? All *your* mum does is gossip about *my* dad. Are you sure your mum's not the mystery blonde?'

'Yuck! She's got better taste than him.'

'What about *your* taste? Have you listened to Hubert?'

'Have you looked at Blake, or just his bank statement?'

'I never realised you were so jealous, Bea.'

'Jealous? Of you?'

She spat that out and it wasn't just the way she said it, or the words she used, but the look she gave me as her eyes went from my head down to my toes and back again – as if I was less than nothing, and well worth leaving alone and the reason why Dad had left. Nothing could be equal to that, not in words. Bea's one look summed up all the insecurities and scars she knew I felt about myself, inside and out. And by scars, I'm not talking about the ones on my knees that I got from falling off my tricycle when I was three! No wonder I never wanted to trust anyone. I couldn't wait to be going home the next day.

As Bea went into the bathroom again, I got dressed double quick and rushed outside. I ran amongst the sheep, did a cartwheel and jumped up and down so much that no tears were ever going to come out. I looked at the sky and thought: God doesn't want me to be unhappy. And to be happy, I have to have breakfast.

Food has a strange effect on me. It stops me being hungry and thus stops the misery of thinking. *Alors.* When I am miserable or *Les Misérables (easy to remember as it's the name of a miserable musical about the French Revolution)* I even forget French.

How To Be Happy

I ran back into the house and was just getting myself to be happy (*joyeux*) again by concentrating on all the good things I know are real, when Blake arrived and kissed my cheek and said he was sorry about last night – *Mon Dieu!*

The sun wasn't even shining – in fact it was overcast and raining – and I should have felt terrible, what with the argumentative Bea, and tonight being our last night, but being with Blake slowly seemed to change the way I felt – like food and willing myself to feel better.

'Where's everyone else?' I asked, as we went into the dining room.

'Hubert doesn't bother with breakfast. Unless it's a live shark to eat, he just isn't interested.' Blake had a way of making me laugh. 'Adults are dead except for Mother, who is up and about somewhere. She runs the entire estate practically single-handedly.'

Mother? It was a different world. I wondered if I would ever call my mum, Mother?

'I wonder if I could ever be as organised as your mum?' I asked. 'I know my mum isn't – she can hardly run to the corner shop without cracking up, or forgetting something.'

'But you wouldn't want to live in the country. You're made for the city, Lily. I wish we lived there – all those models and film stars. Bet you go to film premieres and art galleries.'

'Well, yes, I suppose I do,' I mulled. And suddenly my life seemed as glamorous as Blake's, even if I had only gone to a premiere once, and Mum has to drag me around art shows.

'You know, I've only ever been to London three times in my life, and one of those was a school trip.'

'Are you kidding?'

'No, yes, but it's not hard to kid a girl, or make her happy – you just have to give her a boy, don't you?'

'The answers to all our prayers!'

Blake raised his eyebrows challengingly at me. It was amazing the amount of expressions he managed to pull with just those two bits of hair above his eyes. They could almost have had a dictionary completely of their own. I wondered if there was a book of eyebrow definitions?

I thought about hitting him, but remembered that was rather the opposite of being pro happiness and anti PlayStation games full of pointless killing. I would like to know what adult came up with the idea of making a game where lots of kids get to score points by killing as many people as they can? How could that be fun? It was probably the leaders of the government, when they didn't have enough people joining the army.

The only political party I ever intend to vote for is the Happiness Party. When they invent one, that's when I'll vote. I saw a programme and they do have it as a main policy in Bhutan, which is a tiny country in the Himalayas next to Tibet. If a party is committed to happiness, that is the kind of party I'd be happy to go to. Still the Himalayas are quite a long way to go just for a party.

'As opposed to boys – you just need to give them a few computerised images, in a game about killing people,' I said.

'It's highly complex interaction with graphic cartoons. What girls don't understand is how to suspend their disbelief. It's only a game.'

'Hmm. Very complicated. Girls appreciate the difference between a computerised image and a real person. Can you pass the marmalade? Thank you.'

'We do too, we just like the ones that don't talk. Ergh! You're not putting that on your bacon are you?'

'Yes. Bacon and marmalade sandwiches are completely normal when you think of egg and bacon ice cream. Delicious.'

'Lily, do you just make these things up to be funny?'

Blake was laughing at me, yet even though he was irritating me, Blake's laughter was contagious. He has this little dip in his voice as it goes up and down, like a funny hiccup, and I didn't mind him laughing as long as no one else was around. I hate being laughed at in front of loads of people. When it's just Blake and me though, even when I haven't made a joke and he laughs, it feels like I have.

'It's true! Stop it.' I was laughing myself. 'It does exist, look it up on the Internet.'

'I think that second marmalade and bacon sandwich is affecting your brain.'

'Hmmm, better have another to balance things out then. Can I look at my e-mails on your computer later?'

'Will you need me to help you?'

'No, muppet. Any plans apart from trespassing today? I don't want to be hunted down or starved again.'

'No chance with all your face stuffing.'

'*Charmant. Cochon!*' Swearing in French is much more satisfying.

'You're so sweet when you're angry, and your mouth's full,' said Blake.

'Do you like seafood?' I asked. 'See, food.' I opened my mouth which was full of disgusting half-chewed animal, and closed it, too late for Lady B not to see.

'Having fun?' she asked.

I nodded my head a little too enthusiastically.

'I was telling Lily, there's a little problem with today and any fun. I am officially gated – no trikes, or tractors, even the lawnmower is banned,' Blake said, looking from his mother to me.

'I think a little less adventure might be good for all of you,' Lady B said in a very definite tone.

'What about swimming?' I suggested.

'Great plan, apart from the fact it's raining. Anyway,' Blake continued, 'she said she'd take you and Bea shopping in town.'

'Who's "she", the cat's mother, Blake?' queried Lady B.

'Sorry. Mother is offering to take you two into town.'

'Great.' What else was I going to say?

Hellzapoppy

After breakfast, we went upstairs to Blake's computer

and went in the nursery where Bea was with Hubert, who was back on the PlayStation.

'I told you it would be fine,' whispered Blake. 'All that worrying about Bea not being happy. Look at her, she's completely happy with Hubert.'

Blake looked as pleased as a policeman who'd solved the whole mystery himself. He grabbed me as though to kiss me, and I avoided him. Did boys understand nothing, or was it just this one? This was apparently his proof that girls needed boys to make them happy.

I read my e-mails. They alone could prove how wrong Blake's theories were.

Subject: Lily

Oh my God. Blonde mystery, unravelling like unwanted hair.

Mum has gone and bought a blond wig. BIG MISTAKE. Dad called round to take Bay out and she made me answer the door while she went to put it on – the wrong way round. It would have been funny, if it wasn't so sad. Thought you should know we are living in a state of lunacy, trapped in a mad house.

Come back – all is forgiven. If you get this e-mail . . .
Poppy

Then came this curiosity:

Subject: Me

Something very important to discuss. Can't talk now.
Strange things are happening. Wish I was there too. Didn't
go to Hawaii. Mum and Dad aren't talking. Dad's gone
away and Mum . . . Well, we have to meet asap.

Think our lives are about to be closer than we imagined.
If this sounds strange, it's because it is!

Maya

So I replied:

Subject: Right Back at You

Dear Maya

You can't do this to me. I'm in the middle of nowhere, with
Blake who won't stop playing PlayStation, with Bea who
won't talk to me (cat fight), and with adults who think I'm
stupido. And now you've given me something to go
crazzeee thinking about but that I can't understand. Wata
you try to do to me, eh? Send me to the fruit and nutcase
house?

Confused! Text me.

Lily XXXX

It was all I had time to write before Lady B banged the
gong and shouted for us to join her. And I couldn't keep
Lady B waiting, no matter what was exploding out of my
head.

Facing The Enemy

'Ah, there you are,' said Lady B, as I came down the stairs. 'Where's Bea? I told her we'd be leaving at ten.'

'I'm dreadfully sorry; I'm not sure.'

She gave me a queer look. So I explained, 'I've been reading my e-mails on Blake's computer.'

Just then Bea came running down the stairs. 'I'm ready and here, Lady B.'

'Please call me Cassie.'

'Sorry, Cassie, I keep forgetting. Thank you so much for taking me into town,' she said, so ingratiatingly I was almost sick. Then she saw me. 'You're not coming are you?'

'I thought you'd want to go together. Oh, has there been a bit of a falling out?' asked Lady B. 'Never mind, I'm sure we can soon patch it up – you are best friends.'

'Was,' I muttered, before getting into the car.

After all of Bea's moans and groans about wanting to go junking in a town in the country, getting her to come wasn't easy. Not only because neither of us wanted to sit in the same room, let alone car, but when we were in the car with Lady B, Bea kept looking back at the house where Hubert had been left, like a spaniel separated from its master.

'Now where do you want to go and what do you want

to do? I've got to pick up some things from Hardings, our department store, and I said to Graham that I'd pick up some crabs and samphire for supper tonight, and I've got a visit to make.'

'I just wanted to wander around really,' said Bea, and turned her back towards me for the whole journey, frostily ignoring me.

A short while later we arrived in town.

'Thanks for the lift. Shall we see you back in the car park later?' I asked, trying to sound responsible.

'Yes, good idea. Let's say two-ish. I think everyone at the house is going for a pub lunch, but, if I give you some money, perhaps you could buy some sandwiches or a pizza?'

And before I could tell her not to worry, she'd put twenty pounds into our hands, ushered us out the car and rushed away.

Neither of us wanted to let go of the note.

We stood and just stared at each other, long after Lady B had gone off, dumbfounded by the sheer luck of it. And when luck is so serendipitous, you can't stay angry.

'Well?' I said.

'Well what?' Bea replied.

'I'm sorry.'

'You'd better be!'

'I am! Honestly. I am as sorry as sorry as Surrey, from the heart of my bottom, to the bottom of my heart.'

She looked a little surprised, but the corners of her mouth started to twitch. Then she said quietly, 'OK, I'm sorry.'

'No, I'm sorrier,' I insisted. 'I didn't mean to leave you out . . .'

'Let's forget what we said and did, and go and have a huge hot chocolate and —'

'Find the best charity shop in the whole wide world.'

'Whatever you say, Lily.'

'No, whatever *you* say, Bea.'

'I didn't mean it, about your mum.'

'I know, but I did mean it about your legs.'

'They're not that perfect.'

'They are, actually,' I said, as we walked along the street. 'Do you think we'll always hate each other's boyfriends?'

'Maybe. Maybe it's a jealousy thing about them meaning more than you do to that person?' mused Bea.

'I suppose the thing is, you can't let it get in the way of friendship. It's not like we can only have one friend.'

'But we can only have one best friend,' Bea said. I could have debated the issue, but I was learning what Mum meant when she says that sometimes you really should think before you speak, and you don't have to say everything you think.

Hidden Treasure

We grabbed each other's arms and skipped down the road to some very peculiar looks, but who cared – we were friends again.

The silence never really does last long, whatever happens, however narked we are, because Bea is my best mate – and now we had ten pounds each to spend and that was reason enough to shout, 'Yeha!'

Small towns are very strange, and not only because they are so small. They are a bit like London, but in miniature versions. Not that the shops are smaller, or the streets . . . actually, I take that back: they are. The department store we wandered into to ask for directions had tiny little sections of everything. It was as though Harrods had been shrunk into a dolls' house. There was one counter of chocolates, and one counter of cheese by a bread display, which was next to the stationery that had umbrellas and wellington boots in the middle, with another counter of maps and greeting cards. Socks were even for sale in the cake section.

'I suppose it makes sense to people when they live here,' I said to Bea, but Bea was busy talking to an assistant.

'Excuse me,' she said, when she found one, 'where's the nearest charity shop? Like an Oxfam or Red Cross?'

The young assistant looked at her blankly and said,

'What do you want those for? You can get everything here.' When she saw Bea's resolute face, she relented. 'Turn left out the shop, go down the high street and you'll see it's a short way down on the right.'

She looked at us strangely, all the way out of the shop. We walked along the streets, peering at everything – it was so very different from London. There were no parks in the town, because, obviously, the grass was busy being in the fields.

'Have you noticed how even the doorways are little and everyone's talking to each other?' Bea asked, nudging me.

'I know, it's a bit strange. But maybe not really when you think that their grandparents probably all went to school with each other and they've all known each other since they invented radio.'

'Probably even before that.'

'They must be really, really old. I wonder what we'll be like when we're old. Do you think we'll still be friends, Bea?'

'You betcha. I wonder if anyone here knows my grandparents?'

'Shall we ask?'

'Lily, that is way too random.'

Sweet Charity

Bea saw the shop straight away. It wasn't on the high street, like the girl had said, but it was painted emerald green and at the end of a little cobbled road – you couldn't miss it.

As soon as we walked into the shop, Bea's face lit up as if we had walked into an Aladdin's cave of a sweetshop, or Oxford Street's TopShop with Mega Sale notices everywhere reducing everything.

'Isn't it wonderful?' she said, gripping my hand, excitement racing over her face. 'Look, it's amazing!'

I tried to see what she was seeing, but I couldn't; it didn't look like anything special. It was even worse than that – it looked like Poppy's room when she hasn't tidied it for two months. And it smelled as bad, like a dusty, manky garage-attic smell of a place that suggested any people there would not be living. And from behind the counter peered one of the crinkliest women I'd ever seen. She reminded me to use my moisturiser a little more often, and stay out of the sun.

'Look at these!' cooed Bea. 'And they fit me perfectly. See, Lily, they're vintage original, and these too.'

I could tell she was trying to keep her squeals of enthusiasm down, but it was bit like trying to put a giant cork into the top of a volcano; you knew it couldn't stay unexploded for long.

I looked at her feet and my eyes burst out of my sockets. I don't know much about bargain hunting, but I've seen enough adverts for Chanel and Dior to know that Bea seemed to have one of each design on her feet and they didn't even look worn.

'How much are they?' I asked her.

'Three pounds each or five pounds for two pairs. I'm having them both.'

'Wow!' I said, trying not to think about the dead people's feet they might have been wrenched off.

That is what I worry about with old clothes. I mean, I like the recycling idea about them, but how do you know whether or not somebody's died in them and whether their spirit stays there haunting the new owner?

I'm well aware that not all my thoughts are entirely sensible.

'Why don't you look at the dresses?' Bea suggested.

I was avoiding the dresses – I was already too busy going through a big box of amazing sunglasses: aviators, gold wing tips and huge Victoria Beckham ones. We spent hours going through everything in that shop. And the woman just kept smiling and chuckling at us in the corner, and every time she opened her mouth you could see no teeth, just big pink gums. She might have been a little spooky but, when it came to us paying at the end, she said she hadn't ever seen so much enthusiasm and that we could have everything for twenty pounds!

'Great,' said Bea. 'I love giving my money to charity. By the way, what is the charity?'

'It's for the Hedgehog Refuge Centre.'

'All the better. I love hedgehogs.'

We had loads of stuff; I even bought an amazing ballgown. Now, if there was a posh dinner, I'd be fully prepared. By the time we left at one-thirty, all we'd spent was our dinner money.

'I can see a Red Cross shop over there,' Bea yelped, as we stumbled out of the darkness into the damp day.

'Sorry, Bea,' I said. 'I have to eat something before I die.'

'But you can eat for the rest of your life. Think of the treasures that might be buried behind that very door.'

'OK, but only if we go straight to a chip shop after.'

'What is it with you and eating?' asked Bea.

'Guess you haven't noticed. I'm human: we like to eat,' I informed her.

'Who told you that?'

'Ha.'

'Sorry? Ha? Was that Martian for hello? Or French?'

We knew it was a waste of time as soon as we walked in. There was none of the smell, that swirl of dust, or mystery. It stunk of bleach. Then a woman tried to sell us some rank nylon nightie for ten pounds!

Bea whispered, 'OK, maybe the hedgehog place was just special. This is bad,' she said, leading the way back outside and along the street.

'Oh Bea, does that mean we might eat?' I asked, ever hopeful.

'All you think about is your food. I didn't even have breakfast and I'm not hungry.'

'That is because you are full, full of love for Hubert!' I said, teasing her properly for the first time about the beastie boy.

'Shurrupp. Hunger's only psychological anyway,' she said, and a weird burbling noise rose up from her stomach.

'I think your tummy would like to disagree with you. You don't have to have anything, it's fine. I'll just —' I couldn't continue. My mouth and eyes were watering simultaneously with pleasure. My faithful nose had led us to a small bakery that was brimming full of everything you could ever want to eat.

When the weather is drizzling, you've shopped till you are ready to drop and your stomach's empty, there is only one thing to do. The question was what to eat first. The sausage rolls or the meringues? If it is only the questions in life that are interesting, what's the point in arguing about life? Who cares about parents, my phone ringing, or a text bleeping when faced with a very large chocolatey éclair staring me straight in the eye?

CHAPTER EIGHT

Boy, Oh Boy!

Show And Tell

'So girls, what did you manage to find to do in our little country town? It's a bit sleepy, I'm afraid. I expect you're more used to shopping with your mothers in Sloane Square – Peter Jones, eh?' Lady B was there waiting for us in the car park, loading up bags into the back of the Land Rover but, as soon as we were sitting in the car, she started chatting.

For a parent, Lady B was of the extremely chatty variety, but not in a snooping way like a lot of parents and she didn't ever say, 'When I was your age . . .' Glory be!

'Not really,' I told her. 'I don't go shopping with my mum much, because she's got awful taste in clothes.' I could see I might have said the wrong thing. 'I mean, not for her. She has great taste for her, just the sort of things that she'd want me to wear are a little weird. Bea and I go shopping, sometimes with my sister, Poppy, in Camden or Oxford Street.'

'Ah yes, like Poppy our dog. Hope the boys have remembered to take her for a walk.'

I couldn't stop myself from sniggering. Poppy does more than walk if she's with a boy.

'So did you get anything interesting?' Lady B asked.

Bea looked at me, and I looked at her. How could we tell Lady B that we'd spent the whole three hours junk shopping. Would she think we were poor tramps buying second-hand shoes, even if they were Dior and Chanel? We just smiled.

She saw this and said, 'At least you found yourselves friends again.'

'Oh, we were only ever pretending not to be.'

'Have you thought about being actresses? You had me fooled,' said Lady B, with a smile.

Bea prodded my leg, whilst I tried to keep a straight face.

'We did find this amazing little hedgehog shop in town. So we spent quite a long time there,' I said.

'Selling hedgehogs?'

'No, it was a charity shop for sick hedgehogs. They had

some amazing things. We bought this really old backgammon set and an original 1960s Monopoly board.'

'Almost as old as me,' said Lady B, laughing. 'Dickie likes backgammon. Anything else in those bags?'

'I got a 1950s ball gown,' I told her.

'And I got a 1960s handbag,' Bea said.

'My goodness, what bounty! You did do well. I'll have to have another dig through my old wardrobe and see if there's any old designer stuff you might like when we get back. And of course you must keep that Chanel dress, Bea – it looked so wonderful on you. Strange, I thought you young people just liked new things.'

Bea's face was plastered with a smile so wide it could have burst out the sides of the car.

'Thank you so much, but are you sure?' she said.

'I don't think I'll ever be fitting into it again. Pointless keeping it,' mused Lady B.

'Wow.'

And I must be the most mature person I know, because I didn't even feel a twitch of envy. Seeing Bea so happy was like getting a present myself. Besides there is never a point in being greedy or jealous because it makes you feel sick, and if you feel sick you can't enjoy anything. And if I was jealous, Bea would never lend me the dress. Anyway, how could I complain, because I had Blake. Poor Bea might have a Chanel dress, but falling for hideous

Hubert deserved a big consolation prize.

As Lady B and Bea chatted about designer vintage, another beep from my phone reminded me to look at my texts.

> Best we talk!!! Wo!!! Maya x
> New developments . . . help! M x

The mystery was thickening into a lumpy custard of confusion. If Maya wasn't going to tell me, I would have to practise an unnatural state: patience.

I also had an answerphone message from Mum saying, 'Hope you're having fun, sweetie. Miss you. I'll be there to pick you up at the station as we arranged. Don't worry about us.'

As if I didn't have enough to worry about with NutsMaya! Being told not to worry about Mum just made me do it all the more.

Trying It On

As soon as we got back to the house, we rushed upstairs to put our fantastic treasures in our room, and then we couldn't stop ourselves: we had to try everything on. The ball gown was orange and wild in lots of floating chiffon. It came to just below my knee and had tiny little shoelace straps. It fitted me like a dream.

'Who wears bright orange dresses?' I asked Bea.

'No one apart from you, Lily. You look fantastic, but put your hair up and jazz it a bit and it'll be good. *Très bien, mademoiselle, très bien.*'

'Ah, *merci* bucket, *ma petite tête de chocolat.*'

'I haven't got a head full of chocolate, you nutter,' moaned Bea.

'It's a term of endearment – like calling someone sugarpie or honeybunch.'

'And when was the last time you did that?'

'You'll see. I call Blake that all the time,' I assured her.

'And chocolate head?' she asked.

'Not as often as I should, Bea, but thank you for reminding me. Hey, let's see your shoes!'

Whilst Bea tried on her two pairs of shoes, a cool, blue 1980s mini-dress with weird batwing sleeves and a wide red belt, we danced around, posing. She looked incredible, but then she could wear a jacket potato and look good.

'Shall we go and find the boys and give them a fashion show?' I suggested. I was dying to see Blake and show him my bonkers orange dress and bug-eyed sunglasses.

'No. Let's save it for this evening. We can look really glamorous for our last dinner,' said Bea.

'I can't believe it's gone so quickly. It seems like only yesterday that we arrived.'

And it did. All the days had rolled into one, and all the

feelings I had for Blake had cemented into me believing I'd always felt this perfect way. What was I going to do without arguing and kissing him?

'Actually, it seems slightly longer,' Bea jibed at me. 'But thanks for asking me to come with you. It has been quite fun. Let's get changed.'

And then we bounced along the corridor arm in arm, our new sunglasses like hairbands, pushed into our hair.

'OK, you are desperate to find the boys. What d'ya think? Bet they haven't moved and are still playing PlayStation,' I said.

'I know you're right, sister. So, who were the texts from?' Bea asked in a cheesy American voice and slipped her arm through mine.

'Just Mum and Poppy,' I said. It seemed easier.

'Hey, the sun's come out. Do you think the boys will come swimming with us?' Bea asked.

'Sure.' I said. 'It's a synch. *Ils sont très drôle.*'

'Lily! You know I don't know what you're talking about half the time. Are you sure it's all French, or just crazeeee Lilylanguage?'

I smiled and added mysteriously, 'How will we ever know?'

It's amazing: the true therapy of shopping and friendship. It's not really the buying of loads of stuff; it's the talking about it that's the fun part, the dressing up, the playing. It's like being six and given your first dressing-up box.

Plus Ça Change

'We were right!' Bea and I said in unison, and slapped each other's hands. The drone of the game, with its screeching cars, staccato shotgun fire and occasional burst of music, hadn't changed. The boys remained glued in the same place with the same expressions, still not talking, both hypnotised by the screen of computerised images of people they believed they were running away from, smashing up in their cars or killing.

Plus ça change! It was as though we hadn't even come into the room, let alone been to town, eaten lunch and come back with all our great stuff. And all that time they had just sat there and continued to be potatoes.

'OK,' I whispered to Bea. 'We creep around to the side and we do cartwheels from different directions.'

'Are you sure?'

'It'll disturb them. Trust me. I know how to annoy – professionally, Poppy says. I'm practically the world expert. Then we have to start singing that Lou Reed song, 'Walk on the Wild Side'.

'Really? Like at school? OK. Ready?' Bea asked.

'Steady.'

'Go!' we said together, and we were off cartwheeling

madly and singing the little routine we'd done for a school assembly. Everyone had loved it at school, because we'd dressed up in costumes after we'd seen an old Shirley MacLaine comedy called *Irma La Douce*. We'd borrowed pencil skirts and stilettos out of our mums' wardrobes and smeared ourselves with plenty of red lipstick and drawn heavy Egyptian-style eye make-up on each other all the way up to our eyebrows. Our teachers had been less impressed. They said it was completely inappropriate, to come to school looking like 1950s Parisian streetwalkers. But then they've got no sense of style!

Rejection Issues

We had expected the boys to shout 'Get out of the way' and 'Shut up'. What we hadn't expected was the barrage of plastic bottles and pillows thrown at us, which we caught and pelted back at them. At least they weren't ignoring us any longer. They weren't being apathetic, they were chasing us around the room but for the wrong reasons. Good job we were so fit and healthy. If our parents took to chasing around and jumping over furniture at the same speed as us, they'd probably collapse with massive heart attacks. I expect that's why they take up shouting, so they can do it whilst sitting down and yet still blow up.

'Come here, Lily, you're not escaping punishment,' threatened Blake.

'Oh no, please don't hurt me – I'm so afraid!' I squealed in a really silly, sarcastic voice.

'You wait, you will be. You think it's all funny now, but you won't be laughing when I hang you upside down by your toes from the chandelier!'

'What? Whilst we're having dinner with your parents? I think I might laugh.'

'You think you're so funny.'

'You think *you're* so clever.'

'That's because I am,' he said, smiling smugly, letting me go and jumping back on to the sofa. 'And now, if you don't mind, Hubert and I have our game to finish.'

'Don't be boring. It's our last day to do something,' I pointed out to him.

'You can.'

'With you.'

'Later. Promise,' he said, turning back to the TV screen.

This touched a nerve. Ignoring me, holding the controls (in more ways than one) and speeding back into his obsessive robotic state? I jumped on top of him, just as any other normal girl would, but he pushed me off. This was the last straw! I'd thrown myself at the boy, even puckered up my lips to be kissed and he had landed me a hefty kerplunk on to the floor, on my bum and in front of Hubert, who was laughing. I could see Bea was distraught by Hubert's snubbing technique – you could practically see fumes coming out of her ears.

I got up and tried not to feel utterly humiliated.

'Whatever, Blake. If that's the way you want to play it. Come on, Bea, let's leave the children alone to play.'

Always Have A Back-up

I was mad, and that, by my book, is pretty angry. I slammed his door so hard it bounced back open. Didn't Blake know that I had rejection issues? That's what the family therapist that we all got dragged along to after Dad had left us had said. We stood on his landing.

'Bea, have you got any battery in your phone?'

'Yes.'

'Let's call those boys we met earlier on in town,' I said, loudly enough for Blake to hear and yet think I was whispering. 'They said they were staying just down the road from here.'

Bea gave me a look as if she didn't know what I was talking about, but at least she didn't say anything.

'Oh, it's ringing,' I continued. 'Oh hi, is that Tommy? It's Lily. We met in town earlier? Yes, it was so nice meeting you too. Gosh, that would be really fun. I don't know, it's a little difficult, but you live in London right?'

I reckon Blake had heard just enough to catch my drift as we walked downstairs.

Back in our room, Bea asked, 'What was that all about, Lily? We never met any boys.'

'But if we had . . .'

'You mean you just made that whole thing up?'

'Duh! Yeah, I wasn't talking to anyone, but I think Blake got the general idea. Despicable boys are dispensable.'

'You don't really believe that, do you? I thought you liked Blake?'

'I did, but if he's going to choose to play some rubbish game over going swimming with me, I'll go back to London and find a new boyfriend, and he can stuff it.'

'Hell's bells, Lily, I haven't seen you this angry for ages. Not since, well, this morning.'

'What about Hubert? Aren't you annoyed he'd rather play that game than talk to you? '

'I don't know . . .' Bea collapsed on the bed. 'I think he doesn't like girls. I was right up close to him and he so could've kissed me when I had him pinned to a wall, but he just looked the other way.'

'*Merde!*'

'I know,' she said, laughing back.

'Look, if a boy doesn't fancy you, he'd definitely have to be gay.'

'Thanks, Lily, but I'm not sure that's actually true.'

'Bea, it so is. Hot doggety do! We don't need boys to have fun. Let's go jump in the pool whilst the sun's still about.'

CHAPTER 9

Told You So!

Is This My Life?

'Ah, this is the life!' said Bea, and I had to agree.

What could be nicer than lying on our backs with a warm sun shining down on us in an outdoor heated swimming pool?

The pool had been built into the back of an old walled fruit and vegetable garden. Getting in was like gaining access to *The Secret Garden* – there was a small, flaking dark door, half covered in ivy and warped, which stuck as we tried to push through. Next to us was the dilapidated greenhouse, its window panes shattered and overgrown with a tangle of vines and weeds. It was lovely, in that falling apart way, that I appreciated coming from my family.

Within the garden, autumn flowers were sprinkled around a rolling, overgrown lawn, and a damson plum tree with its tiny dark purple fruit spread its branches wide over a shed.

'That's a damson tree,' I said to Bea.

'Oh really?' she said, not half as impressed as I was. I knew it was a damson, because we'd once gone on holiday in France and there was a tree in the garden and I'd become addicted to eating them, until I was sick. There's nothing like being sick to remember something by.

A couple of pear trees, and an old apple tree grew majestically there too. Fruit still weighed their branches down, and fallen rotten fruit lined the path, all the way to a beautiful old-fashioned pool, which had been covered with a bright blue plastic cover floating on top to keep the heat in and the twigs and leaves out.

Graham had given us the key and told us no one really used the pool, and certainly not after the summer. There was a rolling pulley that Graham had warned us about, so we rolled up the cover as he had said. We'd already changed into our bikinis, so we stripped off our clothes and quickly jumped in the pool.

We expected the water to be freezing but it wasn't at all and, once we'd got used to the fun of jumping into the water and diving off the side of a convenient urn of flowers, we floated on our backs as lazy as exotic flowers, arms and legs stretched out. We stared up into the blanket of blue above with its corpulent white clouds slowly eating up the sky, but the sun still burned its way through. The birds were singing an orchestral racket. I'm not as good on birds as I am on fruit trees, but I know they make a huge noise in the country, when you can't hear anything else apart from the stray zoom of a plane wandering off to sunnier countries.

The Comfort Of Strange Things

'Why didn't Blake bring us here before? I mean, I know the Chinese Garden was sweet and the wood was magical, but this is by far the nicest bit of Blakensold. Don't you think, Buzzy?'

'That's because it's a bit run-down with its rusty watering cans and wheelbarrows. It reminds you of home.'

'Thank you, but I think you're right. All that grand stuff inside the house – chandeliers and posh paintings – it's nice, but you wouldn't want to live there. I mean, not all the time. I'd get tired climbing those stairs.'

'But they like it, and lots of other people would chop off their arms to live in a place like this.'

'What, both of them?'

'Maybe one, and a big toe.'

'What about a leg and a finger?'

This is when I love Bea the most: when we have this pointless sort of conversation, the sort that nobody else will have with me. The kind I try to have with teachers and adults, who just think I'm being silly, when really some of the most silly things are also the most profound, because nobody will have thought of them before. Like chimps being related to us: it's not immediately obvious, until you see them behaving like animals and look into their eyes, and they remind you of all the boys you've ever known. Or all the really good French words sounding so English, as though we already speak French:

ridicule – ridiculous
banal – pointless
bizarre – peculiar
étrange – strange
misérable – miserable.

'If you'd lived here all your life, you wouldn't know any different,' Bea rattled on. 'You'd probably think living in a normal home would be like living in a matchbox.'

'Who do you know that lives in a matchbox, apart from those ladybirds you used to collect? Silly Bea. It's just what you're used to.'

'That's what I meant.'

'So, when you're grown up, and married to Hubert . . .'

'Lily, I refuse to have a sex change to marry him.'

'He's not definitely gay – it's just a guess.'

She looked at me. 'You are joking?'

'OK, I didn't mean *that* Hubert, I meant another one. Will he be really rich and live in a *maison formidable* like this, or will he live in a tiny, poor *petite boîte?*'

'I don't know, I haven't asked him yet. I haven't met him yet. Isn't there anything in between?'

'Well, there might be the chance of a one-bedroom apartment on the Rue de la Rivoli, but I think I'm having that. You could come and stay though.'

'Thanks. And who'd marry you, Lily? And how will Lord Blake feel about it?'

'I think loads of people will want to marry me. Obviously not all at once, but it's nice to think there'll be a choice.'

I tried to imagine for a moment all of this, Blakensold, being mine and it seemed impossible – like looking at a huge mountain, or cliff, and you can't even begin to see how you would climb it.

'I don't like Blake any more,' I shouted out. He'd been rude and even spiteful so, no matter how much I was enjoying his hospitality, *cela m'est égal*, I thought.

If You Hum, You Can't Hear

The wind had started blowing miniature waves skimming the pool's surface, and encouraging goose-pimples all over my skin. The sun was dying for another day and lying on your back, even in a heated pool, can make you quite chilly.

'Let's race for four lengths,' Bea said, just as I was thinking it, so we did. Splashing, laughing, getting warm again and out of breath, we pulled ourselves out of the pool and slid wet as seals on to the old tiles, jumped up and rushed for our towels and our clothes, which we'd left in a little shed.

'We better not forget to put the cover back on the pool,' Bea pointed out.

'Bea, you are too sensible. Let's get dressed first before we freeze to death,' I suggested.

'Let's just do it now.' She marched back to the pool to roll out the cover.

'You are the bossiest, buzziest Bea in humanity, and that is official! They announced it on the news,' I told her. I wound my towel around my waist, so at least my bottom kept warm as we turned the roller to unfold the plastic pool cover.

We were about halfway through, when I heard a suspicious noise. There was a scuffle in the bushes – the sound of someone breathing and a breaking twig.

'Bea, did you hear that?' I whispered to her.

'What exactly, Lily? We're in the country – there's always noise, you're just not used to it.'

I didn't want to look like *un petit imbécile,* so I kept my mouth shut and got on with winding down this hugely heavy thing. I hummed some annoying tune by Barbara Streisand that my mum is always singing along to, just to stop myself listening suspiciously. By the time we'd finished straightening it flat, I was almost dry. 'Right! Now can we get our clothes on, *capitaine*!' I turned towards the shed.

'Yes, Lily, you may, since you've asked so nicely. You're dismissed for the evening.'

'Er, Bea . . . where are they? I left my clothes right here.'

'Eh? Oh, mine are gone too!'

'I told you I heard noises. It's probably the Wild Wooders who've come and stolen our clothes.'

'*That's* sensible. What would a load of ferrets and stoats do with our clothes?'

'I don't know! Wear them for a fancy dress party?'

'Don't you think it's more likely to be the boys?' she asked, as we stood there shivering, towels wrapped around our shoulders like shawls for warmth.

'They wouldn't dare. They would. The scoundrels! Just wait till I get them!'

'That's it, back to the house!' commanded Bea.

'But we're half-naked with no shoes.'

'There's nothing we can do about that, unless you want to wear the wheelbarrow.'

We were forced into the walk of shame. I don't know what was worse: the thought of coming across adults seeing us semi-naked in our bikinis, the deer, or the sheep. It was officially freezing and we couldn't run on the gravel. Our feet were in agony from walking barefoot up the drive.

We went into the house through the back entrance, just in time for Graham the housekeeper, and another man, who looked mightily surprised, to ask us how we were. 'Lovely, thank you,' we replied, dashing up the stairs. The big clock in the hallway showed that we only had half an hour until dinner.

'Bea, we need to make a plan and fast, hop to it.'

Bea helpfully hopped into the bathroom.

'I don't know about you. I need a hot bath,' she said, her teeth chattering.

'We've got half an hour until dinner – it's not worth chasing the boys now. Hey, let's pretend we didn't even notice, and not even mention it until the moment is ripe. It'll drive them crazy. They're just trying to bait us.'

'But how will I get my favourite jeans back?'

'Well, they'll have to confess – we're going tomorrow – unless they want to keep our stuff as mementos.'

'They must give my stuff back, or I'm going to Lady B. Now shut up, Lily, we have to have our baths, and bathing should be a time of rest and relaxation, even if it's only for five minutes. Where have you put my face pack?'

Just My Imagination?

We got our new dresses on just in time, and glided down the staircase together only five minutes late. I wasn't going to miss dressing for dinner. I didn't even care if everyone else was in jeans; tonight I knew my new/old orange chiffon dress looked great. Bea had done my hair up with two chopsticks, but she assured me it didn't look like anyone was sitting on my head eating egg fried rice with sweet and sour pork, so that was all right!

As we walked into the drawing room, there was a more casual atmosphere than the night before. I could tell, because the La Reals weren't covered in diamonds.

I didn't even look at Blake or Hubert. I didn't have to. I knew they were shocked. As soon as we came in, everyone was marvelling over our *fantastique* bargains, and then we showed them the backgammon set, which was even more beautiful than we'd realised.

'That's wonderful, and it's inlaid with mother of pearl and ebony. Look, Dickie,' cooed Lady B.

'I'd like to see that. Can you play? I'm rather a champion of old backgammon, used to play Omar Sharif a few years back, what?' Lord B's ears had perked up.

'Bea's an expert, aren't you?' I said.

'No expert compared to the cat burglar who took our clothes when we were having a swim. Blake, maybe you could solve a mystery and give them back?' Bea smiled so nicely when she said it, it seemed like she was sharing her last ice cream. Not something I've actually ever seen Bea do. She is exceedingly fond of ice cream.

We might have agreed not to say anything, but this was the perfect moment, perfectly executed.

'Blake, you didn't?' said Lady B, outraged.

'No, I didn't. Honestly!' he said, turning a funny pinky red. But not as funny as Hubert. Hubert could have been used as a traffic light, a clown's nose or a tomato.

'Hubert La Real!' his parents boomed. Ah, it was music to my ears. Hubert had been found out. Even Blake was staring at him.

The Joy Of Pain (Someone Else's)

Dinner was sheer bliss, watching Hubert being made to apologise for being so ungallant and rude. He sulked beautifully all the way through the evening and Blake ignored him, along with everyone else.

'I'm sorry, Lily,' he whispered into my ear, after we'd had speeches about what charming guests Bea and I had been, which ignored the whole orchard incident. I asked if Lady B could please write a letter to my father saying that, because I was certain that he'd never believe it if I

149

told him; he wouldn't even believe it if Bea did. I think it is something to do with us not being grown-ups.

Then Bea and I stood up and thanked them for allowing us to stay in their beautiful home and how much we'd appreciated it.

Lord B said we had to sign the visitors' book before we left, as it was part of the ritual of staying there, and then he dragged Bea off for a backgammon tournament. Lady B said that we should come back and stay when Blake's brother, Charlie, would be around. I had seen photos of Charlie, and I hoped he wasn't nicer than Blake because he was much better looking.

'Charlie's a bit of a scoundrel, but he's much more charming than Blake,' she informed me. Just what I didn't need to hear. Blake didn't look happy either. 'So bring your sister Poppy,' finished Lady B. 'They're the same age.'

Damn. Why are adults so ageist? And why am I so disloyal?

Blake leaned over to me and whispered, 'Lily, will you come and talk to me, while I feed the fish?' Then he pulled me by the hand and off through the endless rooms, to a fountain-filled conservatory.

'Now, sit down. Please,' he said.

I sat as obediently as a trained poodle.

'Lily, you know I really like you.'

'Do you, Blake?'

'You know I do.'

'No, I don't actually. You were so nasty to me today *and* yesterday. In fact, ever since Hubert arrived you've been a real . . . well, not very nice at all.' I pouted my best sad pout.

'I'm sorry, Lily. I don't know . . . it's a boy thing. We've been friends since we were little. Hubert doesn't like girls very much.'

'You can tell him from me that they don't like him either.'

Blake was sitting next to me holding my hand and not looking at me.

'You're not really going to meet those boys in London are you?' He was darting these tiny shy looks as though he was waiting for me not to be looking at him. 'I know it's my fault, and you're going tomorrow and I've messed it all up, but I don't want you to see whoever it is.'

I felt sorry for Blake, but I couldn't tell him the boys were fictitious, and I couldn't help myself when I added, 'And we were having such fun.'

'I know.' He looked up into my eyes. 'Do you believe me? I do really like you, Lily. I'm sorry I ruined your stay.'

'*Pas de quoi*. That's French for, "Don't mention it." Except you can, because I know you do like me, Blake, but you are quite, no, very annoying. Even more annoying than me, I suspect.'

151

'Surely not?' he said, and then he started to kiss me. Very softly, at first, like tiny little pecks, and then very unsoftly, until I thought a mini volcano might well have exploded inside my crazy little head.

Boys, eh! *Bonté divine!*

But can they ever behave like real friends? And if boys did, would you ever want to kiss them?

CHAPTER TEN

Return To Sender

The Bisou Alarm

Dear Diary,

What is it about kissing that makes you always wake up early? I sound like I'm a professional kisser! But I wonder if you could invent an alarm clock that kissed you right before you went to bed each night, so that you woke up early in the morning without a squeak, yet fizzy with excitement.

Imagine, starting school like that every day – happy and thrilled!

I remember this feeling at CampMisery with Blake. It was after the first time I had properly kissed him, he patin'd me first, on the very last night, and the next day we all had to go home. Boo hoo.

I had this same feeling, of falling apart happiness, held together with gluey disappointment.

'Yak yak. Nah nah nah, why do you always leave things to the last moment?' Mum's always saying to me, usually ten minutes before school, as I'm doing my homework.

'What is your problem?' I reply.

Hell, it is my problem, if it's MY happiness. Dammit! Hate it when Mum's right! XXXX!

*Sugar!!! Must ring Mum. Wonder if she's noticed I didn't call her back yesterday? Will she understand when I say I was too busy kissing? Imagine what Dad would say: ****!! Bay would dribble out, 'Lala?' Poppy would say she always knew I was a prostitute, or something equally* ridicule et absurde.

Blake. What will I do without kissing him? It will feel like my heart has been slowly squelched through Mum's veggy juice extractor, pointlessly pulped. Hhmm . . . I could go give him a surprise wake-up kiss?

Surprise?

I was up, dressed, packed and going to find Blake, but since it was six-thirty a.m. he might not be that enthusiastic, even if it was me waking him. On the other hand, he might be really happy. But wasn't Hubert up there too? The problem was, I was full of energy, bursting with the delights of life. But he'd said he would come to knock for me. I wondered if I should see if my patience gene was working, though why should it suddenly start? Suddenly Bea farted so loudly, I couldn't help bursting out laughing.

'Why'd ya wake me up?' she groaned sleepily.

'Sssh, I didn't. Go back to sleep,' I said.

Bea rolled over and muttered, I swear, 'Buttersnot.' I tried not to laugh.

I don't know how grown-ups don't laugh when they hear human body grunts. I mean what happens when they're in really important government meetings and the Prime Minister bottom burps? It's not like you can control it. I wonder if anyone has ever invented a de-farting pill? (Is that why the government is always trying to push us to do more compulsory science at school?) Might be worth becoming a scientist just to invent one and become mega rich before living in Paris and Hollywood. How hard can it be? They've already invented the fartless baked bean. I grab my diary so I won't forget.

Must invent anti-fart/burp pill.

But also must pack and look very beautiful, so that I can spend major snog time with Blake before I get on the train to dream about him all the way home. Love is wonderful to dream about, drifting like a feather in a light breeze – though not attached to a bird, obviously.

Blake Loves Lily. ♥ ♥ ♥ *XXXX*

Do You Believe Me?

I closed my diary and put it away in the special pocket in my suitcase and then packed. There were just two tiny problems though, the size of woolly mammoths:

1) What to wear today? I wished Bea was awake for emergency discussion, but if she was I wouldn't be able to go and snog Blake for an hour before she wakes up.

2) Trying to get my bag to shut. I seemed to have a hundred times more than I came with.

I brushed my teeth like a dentist, because *bisou*-ing, let alone *patin*-ing, requires top dental hygiene! Then I wanted to brush my hair a hundred times, but my arm got tired by thirty and I still hadn't decided what to wear. I did discover that I had packed one pair of sneakily hidden white skinny jeans. I squeezed myself into them, over my favourite red polka dot knickers with bows, but my jeans seemed to have mysteriously shrunk! I had to lie down on the floor to do the zipper up. How could that have happened? I found my leopard skin bra (always save the best till last), and a not too grubby fav T-shirt to wear on top. It's one that Suzi, my dad's ex-girlfriend, gave me. I wondered whatever happened to Suzi. She said we were going to remain friends, even though she didn't like Dad any more, but I never heard from her again.

When I'm old, I am NEVER going to make promises I won't keep.

I peeked out between the curtains and saw that the lazy old sun had actually risen (well done my son! Ha ha) and that there was a totally blue sky.

Why I Want To Be A Spy

I used to dream about being a spy, a sort of Jane Bond, but then I realised that what I really wanted was lots of pairs of dark glasses to hide behind. Now that I have three new pairs, I won't ever have to work for the government. Being a spy and going into war zones and getting myself shot at would not be a) glamorous, or b) funny.

Pour l'amour de Dieu et le Republic.

I found my sunglasses, slid them on top of my head, and touched some mascara over my eyelashes. Too cool for school, I was looking well slick – yeah. Sometimes you just have to stand back and admire yourself.

Then I heard a whisper.

'What?' I said out loud. I wasn't scared – I knew it was Blake. He probably wanted to ask me for a pre-brekky snog. Yum. I wondered if I woke him up, just by thinking about him. I do think I am quite psychic, but I don't know if he is. I wonder if I can train him? Imagine the amount you could spend on something else if you just used thought transference instead of a telephone. Love is amazing.

'Come in, I'm awake, Blake,' I said quietly. The handle turned and the door creaked open very slowly. 'Sssh, don't make so much noise. Bea's still asleep.'

I turned around from trying to find my sneakers, when there was no reply. 'OK, Blake, *très amusant!*' I went towards the door to look for him. 'Where are you? I know you're there.' I said to the now open door. 'Blake, you are so annoying.'

There was nothing and no one there. 'Blake?'

There was nothing but a really horrible silence.

A shiver went through me before Blake jumped on top of me and I screamed.

Explaining The Explainable

'Lily, are you all right? I heard you scream.' Blake laughed over mock concern.

'No, I'm not all right. I'm just like Queen Victoria – not amused,' I told him sharply.

'And nor am I!' said Bea, sitting up in bed very unhappily. 'It's bad enough trying to sleep with you, but when did Blake start sleeping with us too?'

'Just now. Lily was screaming,' he informed her.

'I noticed!'

'But it was his fault!' I insisted, then I stopped talking – it was time for action. I grabbed a large pillow and started squealing because I was bashing him with full concentration.

'Hey, hey, stop it for a minute, you two. I need to get dressed and brush my teeth,' said a breathless Bea.

'OK, we'll wait,' I said.

Then Blake grabbed me in an arm lock as soon as Bea

had gone into the bathroom. Cleverly I turned this to my full advantage by kissing him.

'Make love, not war,' I whispered into his ear and exploded a real smackerooni kiss into it.

'Argh! That's not fair. Come here,' he said, trying to grab me.

'All's fair in love and war,' I told him, trying to dodge away, but I was too slow and he grabbed me again and I was butter in his hands – cold hard butter that had been in the freezer, but even butter starts to melt before long.

'Hey, stop that, you two. It's disgusting!' Bea said, coming out of the bathroom.

Only because you're not doing it, I thought, but kept it to myself, and just smiled ridiculously.

'Outside, both of you, outside – you can guard the door. Actually, change of plan. Go into the bathroom and close the door whilst I dress and pack quickly.'

'Yes, Ma'am,' I managed to say out of the corner of my mouth, as Blake kidnapped me into the bathroom.

Save Water, Share A Bath

'What are we going to do in here?' I asked, with a full smirk.

'Well, I've always wanted to share a bath with someone who wasn't my brother,' murmured Blake.

'You have baths with your brother?' I wasn't sure what

I was more scared of – the thought of him having baths with his brother, or with me.

'Not any more, when I was a kid,' he said, sitting down on the side of one of the baths.

'We can't have a bath – we'd get too wet,' I said sensibly, standing my ground.

'Come here, then. Not like that, ow! You could have damaged me for life.'

'What's going on in there?' shouted Bea from the other side of the door.

'Nothing,' I replied. 'I just stood on Blake's foot,' I lied, as I lay next to Blake and we kissed in the very confined space of a large, empty Victorian bath.

Is this the stuff of romance?

'Oh, Blake, I do like kissing you. Do you know that?'

'I just might, oh Lovely Lily.'

Time sped by, or slowed to a full stop, and there was no time or punctuation. It was what was happening, and then it was what was no longer happening. Stopped. Why does having something lovely never last long enough? Why does being miserable or bored go on for ever?

Why do we not have answers to these really important questions? *Pourquoi?* What is the government doing about them?

Bea knocked abruptly like a teacher on the door. 'Stop it now, I'm coming in.'

Damn.

'Can I check my e-mails before breakfast?' she asked Blake.

'You can do anything you want to, Bea.'

'Thanks, Blake. Permission to jump on Hubert's head?'

Blonde Bulletin

'Lily, come here quick. Read my mum's e-mail. The last line.' Bea had come back to interrupt another *bisou*-ing session. She seemed so worked up though that I had to tear myself away and see what Bea had in her bonnet.

Saw Lily's dad with Blonde again. Def not a boy!

I read it, and decided I couldn't care. The plus point was that it couldn't have been Mum, otherwise Bea's mum would have recognised her. Poppy and I were out of danger; all we had to do now was help Mum find her marbles. Most things I lose, I find under my bed. Maybe that was the place to start looking.

The Long Journey Home

Dear Diary,

Time to go home and it's started to rain – properly pour. All you can see out of the window is a blur and splashes of greens and greys. It looks how I feel. All I can think of is Blake. How much I hated him and loved him. Why is love so complicated? I feel like

161

I've forgotten something, like part of my luggage is missing – a coat or something. Leaving him behind is so unfair. It's as if I was made to take off the cashmere cardigan that Lady B had kindly given me. Blake has left his imprint on me in the way that stars do with their hands in the concrete slabs around Leicester Square. We'd spent the whole morning making up for lost time, kissing and hugging and holding hands, and we were only interrupted by Bea.

I would rather not have had Lady B's cardigan than feel like this – so discombobulated. Even using my second favourite word doesn't make me feel any better. I am lost with longing. Gosh did I write that? Lost with longing. That's brilliant. I swear I am such a good writer! Je suis très formidable! Désorienté avec désir. *Everybody said goodbye to us at Blakensold, but Blake and Lady B kindly gave us a lift to Norwich so we didn't have to change trains again. She stayed in the car as Blake helped us on to the train, and he then stayed on the platform waving us goodbye and getting drenched as the rain unkindly pelted him, but he kept smiling and sending me kisses as the train pulled us away.*

Blake did that thing with his eyebrows to make me smile, and I gave in and did manage a smile eventually, because I can't look at Blake and be miserable for too long. I even miss his short, stubbly dog-head hair. Can't think about him too much. Or can I?

Bea is reading Agatha Christie, The 4.50 From Paddington. *She hasn't spoken to me since we left. Why's she in such a stinky mood? Will try and cheer her up.*

'Bet the butler did it,' I said to annoy her.

'What butler? You don't know what you're talking about.'

'I bet it was the butler, with the hammer, in the library.'

'You're getting a book that you haven't read mixed up with a game of Cluedo that we haven't played. Crackpot. And it's spanner or lead piping, not hammer.'

'Bea? Are you going to be a lady defective, when you grow up?'

'Lily, go away and write some smelly poem about Blake. Something like:

Oh Blake I love you so,
I don't want to go.
There's no one like you,
Oh what shall I do,
You smelly old poopoo?

'Your poetry is so bad that you mustn't ever write anything again,' I told her.

'I'm sure you could come up with something equally rubbish. Can't you read your *I Steal a Castle* book? Or have you forgotten how?'

'You are just jealous because Hubert was gay. Blake likes me and is lovely and —'

'And what? What do you want me to say, Lily?'

'I don't know.'

I did. I wanted her to say that I was her favourite person in all the world, but that we didn't always have to be together all the time to be having fun. I wanted her to say that I could have other friends and boyfriends, but that we would always be friends, no matter what. That boyfriends would come and go, but we would always be there.

Instead, my phone beeped the arrival of a text.

Home yet? Call immediately. Maya x
Still on train. Will do. L x

'Maybe you want me to say thanks for a really crappy stay in the country? I could have been having more fun hiring a rowing-boat in the lake in Battersea Park. Do you want me to say thank you, so much, your royal Lilyship, for making me feel rubbish most of the time, because you have a boyfriend and I don't, because you make everyone laugh, and, even if I have got better legs, I'm always the boring, sensible one? Because I'm not going to feel guilty about not feeling the way that you think I should. What do you want me to say?'

'Nothing. I just wanted to chat. But if it's not a good time, I'll come back later.'

'Well, don't because I'd prefer to be in citizenship at school with Mr Taylor! Just let me read my book.'

'OK. That's way harsh.'

And I went back to hiding in my diary.

Dear Diary

Bea is lookey-likey an ugly, bad, hooting owl face. Owls used to be a symbol of friendship. I think she might make a good geography teacher or PE teacher! Next time I'm invited anywhere I'm going alone. Of course somewhere in my heart I love Bea, but not right now. Maybe we need a holiday from each other. Wish I was home. Wish Blake was with me. I suppose Bea's just jealous. I'd be jealous too if I were her – Blake's so gorgeous!

Bored. Really bored. Staring out at this tear-stained window. It's like a painting Bay would do. Am looking forward to going home. Bea would rather be with Mr Taylor – that's ugly!

Minus about going home: Bet anyone a million pounds that Poppy will steal a pair of my new sunglasses in the first week.

Pluses: My own bed, with no Bea in it.

Two-way Traffic

My mobile phone started ringing. What a glorious sound.

'Is that you, Lily? Are you on the right train?' my mum asked.

'Hi, Mum. Yes we're on the train. It gets in at quarter to five at Liverpool Street station.'

'OK, just writing that down. Damn, why is there not one pen in this house that ever works?'

'Because Poppy is the renowned Pen Thief of Battersea

and chews the ends of them so they don't work,' I informed her helpfully.

'Very good. OK, got it. Now did you have a good time?'

'Yes, of course. It was brilliant, once I found my dress!'

'Great, well you can tell me all about it when I see you. I have to go and pick up Bay from playschool now. Byeee!'

And she didn't even moan at me. Either something really bad had happened, or something really good, to divert her mind.

'That was Mum,' I told Bea. 'She's picking us up from the station.'

Bea just nodded her head. I could see she was furiously chewing the inside of her cheek. She always does that when she's annoyed with me.

My phone started ringing again. Maya!

'Lily! Hey, how was it? Did you love him or hate him or kill him? Was he well cute? Chew the beef.'

'Never mind me, did you end up going anywhere, Miss Jet-Setter?'

'Nope. We ended up just going to Paris. It was pretty boring and we had to fly back early because Mum had some business. Really *muchas importante*. Yeah right. I have to tell you now; I can't wait. I think she's having an affair, and it's not with my dad! We need to have a TSD,' she suggested.

That's a top secret discussion.

'OK. I'll phone you as soon as I get home!'

I ended the call and looked up to see Bea staring at me so hard that I closed my eyes and tried to remember all the nice bits of us being away. And then the phone rang *again*.

'Hello?'

'I just wanted to say . . . Well, it was really nice seeing you and I am really sorry about being such a prize git when Hubert was around. Forgive me?'

Blake. Blake. Blake.

'Forgiven, but not forgotten. I suppose I have to make do with your grovelling apologies.'

'Ah, Lily! You will write to me, won't you? MSN when you get home. I mean if you're not too tired? Lily?'

'I was waiting for you to stop talking. I thought you'd rung to hear *my* voice, silly.'

'Well, I did.'

'Well, if you let me speak . . . yes, yes, yes and thank you so much again for inviting Bea and me, BOTH of us to stay, and your family being so generous and nice to us.'

'Don't mention it. Wish you were here now.'

'Me too.'

'Fancy a snog?'

'Hey yeah,' I said, 'but I'd, um, better go. I'll call you later. Love to Poppy.'

'You're not going to see that boy in London are you?'

'What boy?'

'Knew it. Speak to you later, Lovely Lily.'

Bea was staring daggers at me now.

'Wasn't Blake, by any chance?' she asked, and yawned pretentiously.

God, I'll be glad when the journey ends.

I am definitely never, ever, ever going to go on holiday with a friend ever again.

CHAPTER ELEVEN
Not In A Million Years!

David Beckham?

As soon as I got home, I went to my room and called Maya.

'OK, swear you will not tell a soul,' she said.

'OK. What is it?'

'No say it. "I, Lily, will not tell a soul".'

'I, Lily, will not tell a soul. This has either got to be the longest practical joke ever, or really *très bon*.'

'OK. Get ready. Ready? Two nights ago, I was going downstairs to get a glass of milk, because I couldn't sleep after watching this really gross movie about, oh, it doesn't matter. So, I left my room, started down the stairs and I see my mum with – you know I said I suspected she was having an affair? Guess who she was with?'

'George Clooney, the President, the Pope, the Prime

Minister, Mickey Mouse?'

As I rolled out the names, Maya just said no, no, no, no. She was really stringing it out.

'I give up. Tell me, I don't care. David Beckham?'

'No, and you will.' She paused for full effect and then quickly blurted it out. 'Your dad.'

'What? You're telling me that my dad, was in your house, at night, with your mum?'

'Yes.'

'At what time? Are you sure? I mean, are you totally positive it was him? You've only met him a couple of times. You might be getting him mixed up. I mean, he does look like half the men in England, with his sports car and baseball cap, dating twenty-year-olds. Ha! It couldn't have been him – your mum's too old for him.'

'It was him,' Maya asserted. 'I heard him laugh, you know, his weird laugh?'

I was well aware of his weird laugh, not that he did it that often, but I'd pointed it out to Maya. We'd talked for ages about how anyone could have such a weird laugh, and how grateful I was that I hadn't inherited it, because otherwise I would have had to go and join a freak circus: Presenting the Amazing Laughing Lily ha ha ha ha ho.

If Maya had heard him laugh, it was him. There was no way that anyone else could have the same laugh.

I shook my head in disbelief at my father for not only

having wrecked our family (not strictly true because, as Poppy and I always agree, things just got better after he left), but ruining my best friends' families too. Why couldn't he keep his hands to himself? Somehow I felt responsible because I'd told him only a week ago how nice and generous Maya's mum was.

'I'm really, really, sorry,' Maya said quietly.

'No, I'm really, really, sorry,' I told her.

In the end it doesn't matter how many times you say you're sorry if you can't fix it, and neither of us could.

We were silent for a moment.

'Do you think I should tell my mum?' I finally asked.

'Do you think I should tell my dad?' replied Maya.

'Maybe we should speak to them first. I mean I could talk to Dad and you could talk to your mum. How do they know each other anyway?'

'I don't know. Maybe they met when your dad was about and Mum came and picked me up after that sleepover.'

'I knew it. It's *my* fault,' I lamented. 'I can't believe I was thinking that I really wanted to get back home. You just can't trust them. I go away for five days and look what happens. Parents! No wonder Mum's so miserable – she must know. I think she was secretly hoping that she and Dad would get back together, but I made her promise just before I saw you last time that she wouldn't.'

'Do you think they'll stop us being friends? I mean

what's the worst that can possibly happen?'

'We could end up as step-sisters?'

'Dad's going to be, like, so mad,' said Maya.

'Well my dad's been mad for years.'

'I don't mean that kind of mad – I mean angry. Not that he's at home that much.'

'Maybe he's having an affair with someone too?'

'Who? I mean, I love him cos he's my dad, but honestly, Lily, you saw the way he eats.'

'Well look at my dad. You wouldn't want a portrait of him, but your mum's . . .'

'Not very fussy? You can say it. I know. Your dad, my dad. I hope I don't inherit her taste.'

'She's a regular dad magnet.'

'That's not funny, Lily.'

'I know.'

The Mystery Blonde

When I hung up, I realised I hadn't even told Maya about Blake and his mansion and the swimming pool, the secret wood and gardens, his parents and the farmer, my orange dress, let alone how I felt about Bea.

All those things seemed dreamlike from another life, not mine. If I closed my eyes, maybe I could be floating in the pool again, back in Blakensold, friends with Bea, in kissing distance of Blake.

I thought about all Maya had told me; it seemed too unreal to be true. A part of me wanted to go and call Bea, immediately – we always discussed family stuff.

Eventually I went downstairs to see Mum. She looked as low as a tortoise's belly so I put the kettle on and I made her a cup of tea.

'Thanks, love,' she said slipping off her shoes. 'So, Lily, why are you being so nice? Tell me you're not going to say you forgot, and then remembered, that you can't babysit tonight, are you?'

She sounded wobbly.

'No!' I said assertively. Of course I'd remembered – right then when she mentioned it.

'You were talking to Maya, weren't you? Dad hasn't told you, has he?' she asked faux-casually.

Did Mum suspect the affair? What exactly did she know? Though it was very hard, I had to play dumb.

'No,' I said, and I could feel my throat tightening and hear my voice going all squeaky.

'Good. Are you sure? Because it would be sad to spoil such a great surprise.'

I looked at her as though she should be sent first-class delivery to the loony bin.

'Spoil such a great surprise?' What was she on about? Perhaps she had forgotten how to speak English? 'Mum, it wouldn't be a great surprise.'

'Oh, don't tell me Maya's told you already?'

'Of course she has.'

'Oh, what a shame. We wanted to surprise you on your birthday.'

'Well, how very thoughtful of you. Those aren't the kind of surprises I like on my birthday. I like presents and nice things, perhaps even a card. I do not like surprises and you know that, Mum. They make me feel insecure.'

'Well, that won't happen since you know all about it already.'

'But, Mum, aren't you upset?'

'I'm your mum; I have to be brave and as Kahlil Gibran says, "Unleash you like an arrow into the world", and if you like the idea —'

'Like the idea? How could I?'

'But you get on so well with Maya.'

'Odd though it might seem, I like *our* family. Liking Maya doesn't mean I want to be related to her.'

The cat was out of the bag; I'd said it. Mum gave me the oddest look ever.

'Going on holiday with her family for a week over New Year does not constitute swapping families for ever, but it's nice to know you like us.'

I had a feeling of relief and idiocy trickle over me.

'Is that what Dad was doing over at Maya's house recently?'

'Probably. I think he bumped into Maya's mum at his club and dropped her home and she invited you to go with them to Tangier, to keep Maya company.'

Tangier. Wow! Isn't Tangier dark and mysterious? Don't they speak French there? It fleetingly passed through my mind that I had vowed never to go on holiday with a friend again – but I was willing to take another chance, seeing as it was Tangier!

'Now look, you've got it all out of me, you naughty girl. What was the surprise you were talking about?' Mum asked, as she tried to catch Bay. He had finished eating his noodle supper and was madly running around, pretending to be a horse, or a turtle, perhaps even a noodle – you never could tell with Bay.

'It doesn't matter. I was, er, confused with a story I was writing in my book about . . . a mystery blonde.'

'Oh that. That's been solved while you were away. Dad's got back together with Suzi, and Suzi's dyed her hair blond. *Quelle surprise*, as you'd say.'

Poor Mum. No wonder she felt weary at the thought of Dad going back to Suzi. I tried not to show how delighted I was about having Suzi back though.

'Don't worry, Mum, I love you and you don't have to go out with smelly Gilly again. Besides you've got us, you don't need a boyfriend!'

Mum looked surprisingly undelighted by my

demonstrations of mother love.

'Lily, it might surprise you to know that is exactly why I do need a boyfriend; I have to have my own life, otherwise I'd spend my time just nosing about yours. You wouldn't want that, would you?'

'No!' I saw her point. Poppy and I must find her a man.

'So that's why I'm going on a blind date tonight.'

'Isn't that a bit desperate, Mum? At your age?'

'"Frankly my dear, I don't give a damn," as Clarke Gable said to Vivien Leigh.'

'He did?'

'Yes. Now, sweetie, I need to get ready for my date. Do you want to give Bay a quick bath first? Then you could run me a bubble bath?'

'Oh, Mum, that would be great, thank you! I am a sweetie, aren't I?'

'Yes, Lily. Crazy and sweet all mixed up together.'

'Yuck! You make me sound like a portion of sweet and sour chicken.'

'Would you like rice with that? Ha, ha,' Mum replied.

Bay and I were climbing the stairs together, Mum's voice trailing on below us, 'I'll bung some sausages in the oven. Is that all right?'

'Come on, Bay, boboats bathtime,' I said and, just as I opened the bathroom door, I had a horrible feeling that somebody was in there. I quickly shut the door so that

Bay didn't get traumatised by the sight of a naked Poppy.

'Poppy? Is that you in there?' I shouted through the door.

'Bug off! Get out and keep out, pest.'

'Hello, to you too. I have to give Bay a bath.'

'Well, I have to get ready for my date with Nick,' came the reply.

I didn't bother asking who Nick was. Presumably another in a long line of marsupials.

'Leave the water for Bay. You know Mum's going out too?'

'I know, she's got a blind date and you'll never guess who with.'

'Just tell me. Who?' It was too depressing to start another guessing game.

'Well, the good news is it's not Dad. He's got back together with Suzi and that's what Mum was glum about.'

'I know, she just told me.' I tried not to sound too happy, but I was. I liked Suzi. I couldn't wait to see her again.

'Well, she didn't tell you the real, not the really, real, gossip – she's got a blind date with a toyboy.'

'So? He's not younger than Suzi, and can't be worse than Gill . . . is he?'

'It's Mr Taylor from school. Doesn't he teach you citizenship?'

'What? How? There must be a mistake. They've never even met! He's new-ish.'

'Duh! That's how a blind date works! And he's fifteen

years younger than her! Lock up your sons, eh!' She cackled with her usual callousness and sounded like the brain drain she was on this earth.

'How do you know?'

'Because I have spies everywhere. Because he's a friend of some artist friend of Mum's, who's fixed them up. Hilarious, huh?'

Hilarious? Only because Poppy was at Sixth Form college elsewhere.

I lay down on Bay's bedroom floor to die *un petit peu*. Bay seemed to think this was a signal – he got out his plastic doctor's case and began to prod me with his stethoscope. But you know, when real life happens you don't care about minor details like being operated on by a two-year-old with no medical training.

Thank God I was going to Tangier. Maybe I'll be camel-napped and taken to live in a Moorish castle and fed on Turkish delight . . . At least I had something to look forward to.

I would have to phone Bea. Pronto. Oh my dear, dear Bea, why aren't you here, when I need you? How could Mum? I would be the laughing stock at school.

Oh, what an amazing, ridiculous, hilarious, laugh-till-I-cry, dream of a life.

La vie est miraculeux.

The Lilicionary

Translations of some of my favourite French phrases (and my mum's least favourite):

absurde – absurd; unreasonable

allez oop – there you go

un auteur – an author

bécot – peck; kiss

bien – good; well

bisou – kiss

bon – good

bonté divine! – good heavens!

ça glisse comme de l'eau sur les plumes d'un canard – like water off a duck's back

c'était bon pendant que ça durait – it was good while it lasted

cela m'est égal – it's all the same to me; I don't care

c'est dégueulasse – it's disgusting

c'est la vie – that's life

charmant – charming; delightful

compromis – compromise

cochon – pig

désoriente avec désir – disorientated/confused with desire

drôle – amusing; strange

en hiver – in winter

fou – mad; insane

formidable – terrific

ils aiment moi – they love me

imbécile – idiot

j'aime – I love

je m'en fiche – I couldn't care less

je ne m'inquiéte pas! – I'm not worried/bothered. I don't care

je ne sais pas – I don't know

jour – day

joyeux – joyful/ cheery

l'eau en arrière de canard – water behind a duck/water off a duck's back

Lily Lovitt était ici, sur la terre – Lily Lovitt was here, on the earth

ma petite tête de chocolat – my little chocolate head

mais – but

mal – bad

magnifique – magnificent; gorgeous; brilliant

mal extraordinaire – extraordinarily bad

mais – but

maison – house

merde – poo

mon Dieu! – my God!

ne pas – not

non – no

on y va – let's go

pain au chocolat – croissant with chocolate inside

patin – French kiss

partir – to leave

pas de quoi – don't mention it

parfait – perfect

petit – small/little

un petit peu – a little bit

petite boîte – little box

plus ça change! – so what's new?/nothing ever changes

pour l'amour de Dieu! – for the love of God!

pourquoi pas? – why not?

quel choix possible? – what choice is there?

quels les bébés – what babies

quelle surprise – what a surprise

répugnant – regugnant/revolting

rien – nothing

ridicule – ridiculous; laughable

sacré coeur – good grief (lit. 'sacred heart')

sacré bleu – good grief (lit. 'sacred blue')

sauvage – untamed; wild

spécial – special

toqué – batty

tout banal – very trivial/banal

très – very

zut alors! – oh my goodness!

Other books in the *Life and Loves of Lily* series:

Sophie Parkin

Lily is in for a dire three weeks, stranded in the
Lake District at CampHappy with no phone and no
friends. But she's independent and determined, and at
least there's e-mail and a welcome break from her
completely mad family – a mother who hugs trees, a
father whose girlfriend is closer to Lily's age than her
mum's, a demanding older sister, and a small, adorable
and infuriating brother. So camp can't be too bad, can it?

A funny, frank and fresh take on learning to love others,
yourself and some very cute boys. Accepting the bonkers
behaviour of the rest of Earth's inhabitants might be hard,
but '*Plus ça change!*', as Lily would say.
It's not all about learning to camp, you know . . .

Sophie Parkin

Lily has been invited to Tangier with Maya and her
family for New Year. But first she has to cope with
Christmas at home, and a mother who's going out with
her most hated teacher, a sister who steals all her clothes,
and an irritating three-year-old brother.

But in Tangier, Lily faces different problems: Will
she avoid being sold for eight camels? How can she politely
decline the advances of her best friend's boyfriend? Is
belly dancing really the way to a boy's heart? And what
do you do when your mouth catches fire?

It's hard being sane in a mad world! Whether it's her
family, her friends or foreign places, Lily is surrounded by
chaos. Thank goodness she has a sense of humour!

BEST
OF
FRIENDS

True stories of
friendships that
blossomed or bombed

As told to

Sophie Parkin

Friendship can be better than falling in love.

'Some days my jaw would ache from having laughed so much.'
Cathy Hopkins, writer

Or it can break your heart

'I was suddenly terrified that all of our friendship had been one great big lie.'
Flic

And some friendships stay with you forever

'She started to crop up in my dreams, and I did in hers. And that's when we got back in touch again.'
Sophie Ellis-Bextor, singer

Sophie Parkin has talked to teenage girls and high-profile women about the friendships which have meant the most to them. Their stories – affectionate and angry, bittersweet and tragic – show just how much our lives are shaped by our best friends.

☆

www.piccadillypress.co.uk

☆ The latest news on forthcoming books

☆ Chapter previews

☆ Author biographies

☆ Fun quizzes

☆ Reader reviews

☆ Competitions and fab prizes

☆ Book features and cool downloads

☆ And much, much more . . .

Log on and check it out!

Piccadilly Press